More Praise for Peg Alford Pursell

A Girl Goes into the Forest

"The ordinary lives of parents, daughters, husbands, wives, illness and grief are transformed in Pursell's second collection, *A Girl Goes into the Forest*. Here, the lucky reader enters a 'forest' brimming with enchantments, daily life turned transcendent and strange, but no less moving. Assembled like a luminous mosaic of stained glass, these tales read like prose poems—a pitch-perfect condensation of moments, inflected by Pursell's uncanny ear for the lyric. A wonder of a book!"

—Karen Brennan, author of *Monsters*

"*A Girl Goes into the Forest* is nominally a collection of stories, but in its thrilling and original presentation, the book defies categorization. Pursell is a writer of precise and gorgeously riveting images, and her sentences shimmer with the spaciousness and lyricism of poetry. Reading these tales is to be drawn into worlds that feel at once recognizable and mythic. The effect is transporting."

—Marisa Silver, author of *Little Nothing* and *Mary Coin*

"In viscerally powerful stories, Pursell masterfully reinvents the contemporary terrors and wonders that have faced the runaways and the revenants in our oldest tales. Passage by amazing passage, these interrelated stories capture the desiring and sorrowing and believing that can become threatening and then harmless and, at last, fatal. A spellbinding world."

—Kevin McIlvoy, author of *The Complete History of New Mexico and Other Stories*

Show Her a Flower, A Bird, A Shadow

"To call this volume 'slim' would be a mistake. It is rich in the way of poetry—lyric intensity applied to the small wonders of the world—and resonant in the way of music, summoning again and again the mysterious visceral response from its reader. Many of these sentences are running repeatedly through my mind, like noteworthy and unforgettable songs."

—Antonya Nelson, author of *Funny Once* and *Bound*

"A gorgeous parade of narratives where every sentence is an insight, and every paragraph a mosaic that turns broken shards of language into poetry. I read *Show Her* the way you read in a dream, the way you see that flickering in the corner of your eye which means you're haunted. Highly recommended."

—Glen David Gold, author of *Carter Beats the Devil* and *Sunnyside*

"What a pleasure to read *Show Her a Flower, A Bird, A Shadow*. In story after story Pursell creates vivid characters and piercing situations. Nothing is too small for her imagination—a wren on a branch, a hole in a sock, ginger tea—and nothing too dangerous—a girl hit by a stone, a mother and daughter struggling. In a matter of a few words, a few lines, Pursell transports us into vivid situations of loss and longing. This is a dazzling and lovely collection."

—Margot Livesey, author of *Mercury* and *The Flight of Gemma Hardy*

"With precise beauty and unsparing wisdom, Pursell shows us 'Anything can happen: anytime.' The dead resurrect in fragments of memory, kindness is necessary courage, lives dissolve, reshape, renew, and another's hand will imprint on us its lesson in brokenness or its blessing of love as we fly into and out of the cages of our temporal selves. *Show Her a*

Flower, A Bird, A Shadow is a small but fiercely sacred book, immense in its gifts."

—Melissa Pritchard, author of *A Solemn Pleasure* and *Palmerino*

"What intense bits of insight these are—dramas, both painful and lyrical, are captured in these superb concentrations of prose, with their flashes of brilliant detail. An original book, with a long, shimmering after-effect."

—Joan Silber, author of *Improvement*

"I've always firmly believed that the amount of words a story contains has zero to do with how much weight the story carries. Pursell's new book, *Show Her a Flower, A Bird, A Shadow*, proves this once again, and proves it in spades. These stories are like gut checks to the soul."

—Peter Orner, author of *Am I Alone Here?* and *Love and Shame and Love*

"Pursell writes beautifully and evocatively about both the world around us and the one within. Her prose is spare, her observations keen, her heart fully on display. *Show Her a Flower, A Bird, A Flower* is striking debut from a great new writer."

—Tom Barbash, author of *Stay Up With Me*

"Reading this book is like walking through a snowfall of petals—and thorns. There is a light airy feeling to Pursell's delicately worded fragments that is seductive, at first, until you realize that each swirl contains small stabs of loss and pain and violence. A really beautiful, unique collection."

— Molly Giles, author of *In All the Wrong Places* and *Iron Shoes*

A GIRL GOES INTO THE FOREST

 *stories*

PEG ALFORD PURSELL

DZANC
BOOKS

DZANC BOOKS

5220 Dexter Ann Arbor Rd.
Ann Arbor, MI 48103
www.dzancbooks.org

Library of Congress Cataloging-in-Publication Data

Names: Pursell, Peg Alford, author.
Title: A girl goes into the forest : stories / by Peg Alford Pursell.
Description: [Ann Arbor, Michigan] : Dzanc Books, [2019]
Identifiers: LCCN 2018051973 | ISBN 9781945814877
Subjects: LCSH: Love--Fiction. | Loss (Psychology)--Fiction. | Short stories,
    American--21st century.
Classification: LCC PS3566.U688 A6 2019 | DDC 813/.54--dc23
LC record available at https://lccn.loc.gov/2018051973

First US edition: July 2019
Interior design by Michelle Dotter

Printed in the United States of America

10   9   8   7   6   5   4   3   2   1

CONTENTS

~ONE~

HOW FAR SHE HAS COME IN THE WIDE WORLD SINCE SHE STARTED OUT IN HER NAKED FEET

~TWO~

SHE LOOKED BACK THREE TIMES BUT NO ONE CAME AFTER HER

~THREE~

SHE ONLY DABBLED IN MAGIC TO
AMUSE HERSELF

~FOUR~

NOW HIS GAMES WERE VERY DIFFERENT
FROM WHAT THEY USED TO BE

~FIVE~

IF SHE DIDN'T LIKE IT THERE, WHY, THE WORLD
WAS WIDE, AND THERE WERE MANY OTHER
PLACES SHE COULD GO

~SIX~

HE TRIED TO SAY HIS PRAYERS BUT ALL HE COULD
REMEMBER WERE HIS MULTIPLICATION TABLES

~SEVEN~

SHE KEPT ON SMILING, AND HE BEGAN TO BE AFRAID
THAT HE DID NOT KNOW AS MUCH
AS HE THOUGHT HE DID

~EIGHT~

HOW EVER DID YOU GET LOST ON THIS BIG SWIFT RIVER, AND HOW EVER DID YOU DRIFT SO FAR INTO THE GREAT WIDE WORLD?

~NINE~

THE LITTLE GIRL, WHOM SHE CARRIED ON HER BACK, WAS A WILD AND RECKLESS CREATURE

She said, "I am groping in the dark."

—Muriel Rukeyser, "Käthe Kollwitz"

She felt as if she were standing on the edge of a precipice with her hair blown back; she was about to grasp something that just evaded her.

—Virginia Woolf, *The Years*

Well, she was an American girl
Raised on promises

—Tom Petty

For all my girls
and in memory of Kathleen Lees Lloyd

A GIRL GOES
INTO THE FOREST

T ENTATIVE, CURIOUS, UNCERTAIN, ALIVE, she followed him into the woods, moving in the direction where perhaps she imagined the rest of her life waited. So ready for something to happen. The old secret cottage had fallen to the ground. He acted as if that surprise were inconsequential, and spread a thin jacket over the dark forest floor. To lie down was harder than it looked to be; wasn't everything? A thick scent of pine needles. Sour smell of mildewed ash. The moon rose. White and tiny, smeared into the fork of a naked branch overhead. Wind chattered like teeth through the trees, their trunks storing hundreds of years of memory. In this new dimension of light and shade, she lost track of who she'd been before, of the home in the town with cracked streets, concrete and glass, sun-scoured spires. Beside her, he said nothing. A troche on the tongue of the needful earth, she lay, thick thirsting roots deep underneath. This was something for the body to feel. There is so much for a body to feel before it goes, returns to its simplest elements: carbon, hydrogen, nitrogen, sulfur. Full night must eventually come on, its deeper chill. They might remain. Together. It might turn summer and she'd have survived the season. Or the earth might be soothed, some want eased.

～ONE～

HOW FAR SHE HAS COME IN THE WIDE WORLD SINCE SHE STARTED OUT IN HER NAKED FEET

OLD CHURCH BY THE SEA

I HADN'T VISITED THE abandoned church by the sea in many years, not since that day with my teenage daughter. She'd reached that age of awkwardness, so painful to watch, when people had begun telling her to calm down, to lower her voice, to walk, not run. I'd brought her to this bewildered Eden: huge boulders in the garden, cold shadows, the infinite space of sun. Sad jasmine crawled everywhere, even over the dilapidated fence deteriorating as if the weight of the flowers caused its demise. I'd imagined we would run and play as in a game of tag, like we had when she was younger, as if we were two butterflies in the tall grass.

She wore dark glasses and sat on a stone bench where a white cat lay sleeping. I didn't dare believe she was looking at me behind those lenses. Her chin tilted up, and I decided she was examining the distant countryside: yellow grass spread with repeated cows, the bay a shimmering backdrop of monotony. A quick wind stroked my bare arms and prodded dark clouds across the sky. It began to rain.

We made the long drive home in silence, her ear buds in place, the tinny chords of her music reaching me behind the wheel. We neared the close-by village where at the street corner, under the overhang of the roof of the grocery mart, a group of five men sat as if hypnotized. My daughter's head abruptly swiveled, stayed fixed in their direction until we made the turn and left them behind.

How the imagination can forge something from a moment!

Here now the burning light of day rested in all its blue brilliance on the lone remaining stained-glass window of the church, miraculously intact. The sun bleached only the tips of the wild grasses, while closer to earth, darkness churned like sea reeds. Heavy clouds clung to the distant hills speckled with their animals.

Inside the old church, it was almost possible to hear what people do to one another.

I always think I'll circle around to the exact explanation for what went wrong. Having and wanting at the same time—that's what it was to carry my daughter inside me. After, I was emptier than I could ever have imagined, I thought then. Then, when I thought I would have the chance to tell her one day.

SMOKE, MUST, DUST

I N THOSE DAYS WHEN we entered a store or a restaurant, my seven-teen-year-old daughter and I, we received a variety of looks from the clerks or waitresses that ranged from cautious to uncertain to suspicious. She and I were always in opposition, barely managing to tamp down the conflict when others neared.

I scoured literature on parenting, consulted family counselors, listened to relaxation programs through my headphones.

She was a brooding beauty who wore a graying white rabbit fur jacket that she'd found at a thrift store with tiny skirts and thick-soled dark leather boots, and dyed her hair unnatural colors, blue, red, green. She knew that smoking cigarettes would harm her, that I didn't want her hurting herself, but she smoked brazenly, and I didn't say much, fearing the many other ways that she could damage herself, and maybe did.

The day she turned eighteen, she was gone. I'd felt that departure coming all along, but the sight of her empty closet took the breath out of me. I fell to my knees, the carpet harsh against my face, filling me with an amalgam of smoke, must, dust.

I lay there while the sky outside the windows passed from metal gray to black.

When at last I learned that she'd traveled across the country to live with her father, I pictured myself curled up on her bedroom floor that day and was relieved she hadn't witnessed my collapse. I called her father to make certain of her well-being, and in the days that passed before he returned my call, memories of him churned. Images of a man who'd set his mouth closed against anything that might seep out of it without his approval. His critical, watchful nature. The sense that there was someone inside that hard body unknowable, someone I wouldn't take heart in knowing, had I been able to.

His voice on the phone testified to the accuracy of my memories. He had no idea where my daughter was now. She'd come and gone. I'd done a lousy job with her. What a mess. Showing up on his front step like that.

I think there's something unacknowledged about survivors. It's possible to want to be too good at it, survival.

When I think of my daughter now, I feel she was braver than me, never afraid to go too far.

What should we do with the rest of our lives?

What should I do?

A MAN WITH HORSES

THE DAY BEGAN WITH beauty, with happiness. After years of saving, I'd brought my daughter to the bungalow by the sea where we'd always wanted to spend a summer. She'd graduated from high school two weeks before, so I'd just made it—our last true time together before she went to college. I laced up my running shoes, left her sleeping in the pleasing cottage, and set off for a quick run. I crunched down the shell driveway, salmon colored in the dawn, onto the oleander-lined path toward town. The humid air pressed my skin, but a breeze blew in from the ocean. I was contented, even triumphant. The arched sky was so blue it was hard not to believe in something grand behind it, behind everything.

I passed through the small town center, where laundry fluttered from the balconies like pastel ghosts. I was someone who had to work harder than others at love, I knew that, even with my daughter, who had always seemed, from the start, too clever to choose comfort. When she was an infant, the knowledge that I alone was the only solution to her troubles was excruciating. But somehow, we'd made it through, and she was on the verge of making her own way in the world. I imagined talking deeply in the days to come, learning what made her feel empty, what made her full.

I turned the bend in the road for home, the sun lighting the red tin roof and sparkling the distant caplets of the sea. As I neared the house, I saw a black car I didn't recognize in the driveway and began to feel afraid. I didn't know why.

On the porch, a large man with a tanned face, eyes hidden behind dark sunglasses, stood beside my daughter with her pale face, so close to her that he must have smelled her golden hair, the lingering sweet verbena scent of her shampoo. Near my daughter's feet sat her new suitcase. Her eyes watched me carefully.

The man took her elbow in his enormous furred hand, and she told me that they had been secretly married the previous weekend, that they were moving to Chile where he raised horses.

While there was no knowing what was true, I knew there was no stopping my girl from doing whatever hard thing she was determined to do.

Certain men are glad to find certain girls. The more unbreakable the girl, the better. This girl, no, had never wanted contentment. I placed my hand on her cool cheek, so soft. She closed her eyes against the feeling.

THE OLD CAT
ON THE COUNTERTOP

WHEN SHE BIRTHED HER daughter, the love that had been dammed up inside her immediately flowed, a warm stream of exquisite tenderness. Everything she looked at was beautiful, bathed in clear light, even the dun-colored curtains that enclosed her hospital bed. She never forgot the incarnate feeling, that sensation that a part of her own life had just begun, that everything that had passed before was at once forgettable.

Last night she and her daughter, now a young woman, had had another fight. She'd been out of herself, someone else, who'd hurt her daughter, the two of them grappling in the kitchen at the top of the basement stairs. Their old cat watched from a spot on the countertop where the animal wasn't permitted to be, whiskers up and unmoving. Neither mother or daughter had been who they thought themselves to be. She'd slapped her girl. How to reinhabit herself, a tight, foul-smelling shoe lined with fear and remorse she would have to journey in, wishing for a beacon promising forgiveness.

The old white cat sat barely blinking while she rinsed breakfast dishes. Invisible dander invaded the kitchen. Blisters would form, burst, scar. Agony to remember such a moment when everything was shot with beauty. The cat leapt to the floor and disappeared.

IGUANA

HER HUSBAND LEFT HER sitting at the little table at the edge of the garden under the overcast sky, exasperated with his role of the odd man out. She sensed a truth in what he said, felt relieved when he retreated into the house. She preferred her own company when overtaken by this longing, her mind noisy with remorse. On the garden fence, a green iguana, bright as neon, stopped climbing. She dared not turn in its direction.

Cultivating peace demanded solitude.

You need life and explosions, her husband disagreed. But by now he'd learned that nothing could dissuade her from her need to be with herself.

The iguana was a model of stillness under the darkening sky. The border of tall grasses, full as the skirts of Victorian ladies, rustled in the breeze. The iguana remained motionless. Her daughter had inked a ring of like reptiles around one ankle, a bright green tattoo. Perhaps the green had dulled by now.

As a young girl, her daughter had danced like no other, her powerful legs lifting her from the ground, a pinnate soul in flight.

She'd once made for her girl a necklace of bones and beads that sparkled at the base of her willowy neck.

No one can deter a person from her mistakes.

Recently she'd gone to see her daughter perform in a nearby city. After the show she'd called to her daughter across the parking lot, hurrying to catch up before the young woman climbed into the van. Her daughter's surprised face turned to her, clouded with secrets and dark loyalties. The red scarf tied at her daughter's throat slipped to reveal bruises, and when her daughter caught her eyes looking, she nodded, barely, before stepping into the van, not one word spoken.

It's better not to talk sometimes, I believe that, she'd said to her husband on occasion.

That was probably true.

She turned her head and the iguana vanished. Quiet reigned. She lifted her face to the sky. She wanted rain to mist her face, wash down her neck, thrum on her throat. Water she could wipe away.

ASTRONOMY AT
DESERT SPRINGS

I N THE COLD AND burning night of the desert, the astronomer explained the sky, allowing each of them, husband and wife, turns at his high-powered telescope. To focus, she had to close one eye. Before they'd met at the appointed hour, the guide had advised them to dress warmly, and she thought she had, but the clothing (long sleeves, down-filled vest) wasn't enough, like so many things lately.

Their guide pointed to a milky cluster in the sky, explained the myth of a ladder amongst the stars. The space of the viewable universe hierarchical, tiers of light years layered to the unknowable. Back at the hotel, her knitted blue cap lay forgotten on the bed. In the room where they'd fought, another rung lost. Her ears flamed with cold under the glittered sky, her fingers in her pockets, blunt instruments she couldn't bring to the telescope at her turn.

She spoke to say she'd been wrong, so unprepared, she had to go back. Her words, tiny in the deep night, were rewarded with the quietude, then the sigh.

UNKNOWN ANIMALS

HE WAS SMILING DOWN at her, his full lips, eyes shining, so happy to have had his say. Above, stars littered the black, black sky. Somewhere in the distance, the unheard ocean.

She lay on her back beneath him, the ground cold. Once she'd loved these camping trips, the open salted air, shifts in the wind offering the smell of the extinguished fire's ashes, scents mixed with the briny taste of his skin. The excitement of animals lurking out there in the surrounding darkness.

His face had been so dear that she knew every crag, every line, how his eyebrows quirked when he was unsure. Her knowledge of the intricacies of his changing expressions, the minute shifts in the muscles along his jawline, had elated her.

Now as he fingered his beard, she filled with the sense that not only was it he who was ugly, but she too. Only momentary beauty existed, an instant of respite with the sole purpose of demonstrating its elusiveness.

It was no one's fault that she lay as she did, stiller than she had heartbeats earlier, the hardness under her back unforgiving. Love was like rainfall, either softening the ground or washing it away.

His say—those insignificant words he'd insisted upon—drifted away in the night.

His smile evaporated. She let him take her hand once he moved to lie beside her.

Soon he fell asleep. She listened for animals out there in the wilderness, for any sign at all.

⟨⟨ TWO ⟩⟩

SHE LOOKED BACK THREE TIMES
BUT NO ONE CAME AFTER HER

GOODBYE,
ROLLER COASTER

WE STOOD ON THE brick sidewalk in front of our dark house, watching the fairgrounds burn to the ground against the backdrop of indigo night, feeling the flaming orange heat from half the town away on our faces. If you don't take chances, said the man in the black-and-white-striped pajamas, you might as well not be alive. We thought they were pajamas, though they looked like something we'd seen Larry, Moe, and Curly wear on an episode of *The Three Stooges*, chains with heavy metal balls attached ringing their ankles. We'd heard Janis Joplin sing an old blues song about a ball and a chain on an electrifying album, music like nothing we'd ever heard before, and as we listened, the Three Stooges' costumes may have flashed through our minds, but probably not. It had been 1975, Dad had a new stereo and lots of record albums, and we thought we knew how to dance, flinging our bodies around in space behind the closed door in our bedroom, breathless, laughing until we cried.

The man wearing pajamas lived on the block, that sagging wooden house on Sycamore Street. But pajamas? We'd never seen a grown man wearing pajamas. Dad had left a black-and-white flannel checked bathrobe, never worn in our presence, hanging in his closet. We would grow up and leave our house and what would happen to that robe? We stood watching the fairgrounds burn to the ground against the backdrop of indigo night, feeling the flaming orange heat from half the town away on our faces, the brick sidewalk under our feet, the dark house behind us. What was the emergency that the man couldn't have dressed? We wore shorts and T-shirts and flip-flops.

Our attention went back and forth from the fire to the man, shiny black slippers on his feet, a tremor in his body. We would never go to the county fair again: goodbye, bulls, horses, pigs! Goodbye, roller coaster! No one acted as if they'd heard what the man in pajamas said when he said it: If you don't take chances, you might as well not be alive. He shivered in the night: we saw that in our peripheral vision. Cold in his flimsy pajamas, or incensed by the drama of the rising flames, or so alive, loose and free in his pajamas in the neighborhood. The brick sidewalk under our feet, flaming orange heat on our faces against the backdrop of indigo night, we watched the fairgrounds burn, the roller coaster leaving us, the dark house behind.

DAFFODILS

THE FIRST SATURDAY OF spring, the brother and sister, ten and nine years old, sat on top of the picnic table at Lake Rhonwen on the other side of town from home, where nothing good could take place. Forgettable pebbles lined the steely water. The sun had come out. Clumps of frozen snow still clung to the bare ground under the firs in the distance. Stands of misshapen daffodils, cloistered on a strip of muddy ground nearby, bent in the wind that had picked up out of nowhere. The flowers had been brilliant and happy, but now, beaten by the winds, were pale, sorry.

The brother jumped down from the table and picked up a long stick. He headed to the daffodils, and the sister screamed. He turned to face her and scowled. Don't act like you know what I'm going to do. You don't know me.

She repeated what her mother said to her: she could read him like a book.

He laughed. You can't even read. He took a step in her direction and waved his stick.

She looked away. Disengagement was her only defense, and sometimes it worked. Better the heads of the daffodils than hers.

She left the picnic table, the lake, and started the trek home, her legs feeling thick and tired. The sun had vanished entirely.

Trudging up the long hill pulled the breath from her ribs, and her eyes smarted in the cold. Once she crested the hill, the sidewalk would begin and the remainder of the walk through town would be easy. This was how you did it, one step at a time, telling yourself you could reach your destination. You could. Her red hands were growing numb.

Her brother's voice in the distance called her name.

She half-expected that any moment he would come up behind and whack her with the stick. She looked back. In his hands he carried a bouquet of the long-stemmed daffodils, dazzling in darkening sky. She wanted to cry.

The wind cut through her, and her teeth chattered while she waited for him. It would be easier to crest the hill together. With the lovely flowers.

He neared, his breath gray clouds before him, and she reached out for the bouquet, words of thanks on her lips.

AN UNCLE

AN UNCLE IS A babysitter in a pinch, which happens rarely, only when Mother has to run out to comfort her friend Suzanne, an emergency that isn't *that* rare, in Dad's opinion, but an uncle is someone who doesn't take sides in the matter. He comes to the rescue, and sits on the sofa watching a wrestling match on TV, and says *Stop it now!* after you and your sister have slapped each other's arms blazing red with your Barbie dolls. He gives you a look that makes your stomach heavy and you feel pretty sure he knows you're to blame—you're the oldest. You sing all the Beatles songs you can think of, to impress him with how you know the words to so many songs. He's like your dad in the way that he stares straight ahead at the action on the screen. You brush all your hair from the back of your head forward, smooth it down over your forehead, past your eyebrows and into your eyes to look like Ringo, who isn't the cutest Beatle but has something special. "Look, Uncle Lew!"

He glances over and gives a snort, and you feel a little better.

An uncle is someone your mother likes a lot, and when he drops by unexpectedly, she turns off the iron and sits down with him at the kitchen table, where they drink Pepsis or RC Cola, if it's on sale at the Shop n' Save, and eat chocolate macaroons, and his voice flows low from out there, and she giggles. There is something high and twinkly about that laugh, like the sound of the glass wind chimes suspended outside the neighbor's door. You wish you could talk her into buying chimes to hang on your porch. But some day. When you grow up and you live in your own house, then. Then.

An uncle is someone your dad doesn't mind loafing around with, as long as Dad's work day hasn't pushed him right to the edge, though when the two of them are together they don't say much, they just sit, in aluminum-framed lawn chairs under the maple tree, where darkness falls as they put away a six-pack of Pabst, the click-swish of the tab pulls perforating the silence, the red-hot tips of their cigarettes dotting the night.

He's a guy who looks like your dad but also different, and though your dad is actually sort of handsome, your uncle is good-looking in a different way. Suzanne says he looks like Elvis Presley, but Elvis Presley doesn't wear glasses and you don't see the resemblance, but there's no one to share your opinion with because, in fact, you've been listening in again when you should be minding your own business. Your sister would rat you out in a heartbeat.

An uncle is a guy who doesn't bring you gifts since he doesn't have money and since probably no one has ever told him it's okay to give presents. He's someone who doesn't ever seem to notice you're changing, you're changing every day. He's someone who seems to see a you that might be you, but is not the you that's standing right there before him, while he pores over the sports scores in the newspaper and Mom arranges the candles on your birthday cake.

He's way younger than your dad and there is something a little exciting about that, that he's closer to your age than your parents', that he's still a teenager, just nineteen. Everyone wants to be a teenager. It's the most exciting time ever, this is so obvious, and the idea that you will be—it's only a matter of time, four years!—is thrilling. And terrifying. How will you know how to handle yourself? How will you learn the dances? Should you wear lipstick each time you leave the house—is there even going to be lipstick in the future? When you watch *The Jetsons*, with Rosie the robotic maid, who you sure could use in this house—no more setting the table and drying the silverware—you understand that everything is going to be different. But say that lipstick does still exist. And you are wearing it when you kiss a boy, which of course you will sooner or later. Will the boy hate the taste of your lipstick, and what if it makes him throw up?

You wish you could ask your uncle a few questions. But he is someone who is going to act like an adult, particularly since he is the baby of the family, as Dad says, something he hates to hear, you can tell, his face red, hands shoved into his pockets or laced behind his head as if the remark is nothing but a little pest buzzing by, not worth the effort to swat away.

He's someone who doesn't have any choice—he's going to have to go into the war—but if Grandma hadn't babied him all his life, he wouldn't be so afraid! When you see the war on TV you think you would be very afraid, and though you are a girl, it is hard to believe that a boy, even if he's older and everyone calls him a man, can feel so much different than a girl. When does it happen, when does it start, a boy feeling different than a girl? Does something go off inside, like a time-release capsule, that makes a boy no longer scared of what frightens you?

An uncle is someone you try to figure out, sneaking glances at him when you're sitting in front of the news on TV, all those palm trees and fiery explosions bursting on the screen. The war is loud, terrifying.

He's someone who, before he ships overseas, comes for a picnic in the backyard. Mom bakes him a devil's food cake with whipped-cream frosting, Dad cooks super-burgers on the charcoal grill, everyone's paper plates *groan with food*, as Uncle Lew puts it. He says that in a bright voice and everyone laughs.

The picnic under the maple tree goes on and on, no one saying a word, and you wish you could think of a fun thing to say. Then you have to go to bed, and you give him a hug, something you have never done, and the cool skin of his arms in the hot night is something of a shock, and you say *Good luck!* because what in the hell is the right thing to say. You feel perfectly justified thinking the word *hell.* In your bed you think *hell, hell, hell,* and listen hard for anything the adults might say, still gathered in the dark under the tree. The only sound that floats through the open window is the chirr of a lonely cicada.

An uncle is someone who, when you see the headlines in the newspapers, you try to picture in that swampy place, booby-trapped with bombs, him in a uniform and a helmet, his glasses on his sweaty face. What would happen if his glasses broke? How would he see to save himself? He's someone who pushed a button up his left nostril when he was a kid, your grandma told you that, and the button didn't come out for months, and she wonders if that was what caused his respiratory issues. If that has anything to do with how his lung collapsed over there. He's fine now, he reports, in his letter that lies in her lap. But the thing that worries Grandma is how long it takes to receive the letters. Who knows if this is still true, if he's still fine, if something else could have happened since?

You wonder what his handwriting looks like on the letter but you know better than to interrupt. And this night staying over at Grandma's—which is a new experience, but she is lonely and you are the oldest—while you are sleeping in your uncle's room, you stare up at the pictures on the walls and think about how he used to stare at the same pictures, and isn't that just so strange when you have never even seen his handwriting. The pictures are of pixie-like creatures with enormous eyes, and you have to wonder if he really liked them or simply put up with what his mother picked out, the way you have to put up with what your mother picks out for you. Another thing you can't ask him.

Say that you could get to the post office and buy some stamps and someone would give you the address—is that what you'd write in your letter? Maybe he wouldn't like to hear you'd been in his room. Maybe he would think it's weird the way you think it's weird, that both your heads have lain on this same exact lumpy pillow with its musty smell that makes it hard to fall asleep, but which maybe he never smelled because of his respiratory problems.

An uncle is someone who likes his eggs scrambled, you find out from Grandma in the morning, and doesn't turn up his nose at a glass of cold milk with the creamy yellow surface. He knows it's good for you, for God's sake! He's someone who'd be glad to take a break in the hammock quietly, and wouldn't squirm around and fall out and practically give her a heart attack with all that howling. He would probably not approve of your selfish behavior—like your parents do not approve when Grandma takes you home early and has to miss her stories on TV.

An uncle is someone who does come home from the war, his face tanned but also somehow pale, who seems bigger, with muscles, but also shrunken at the same time, you can't say how. He wears different glasses now, wire rims. And he has money. He's someone who returns with gifts, a reel-to-reel tape deck for Dad, delicate pink china with hand-painted flourishes for Mom, kids don't count. He drives a white convertible sports car with a flashy silver logo of a wild pony on the trunk.

An uncle is someone who's around more than ever for a while, while he's getting his bearings, Dad says, but he speaks less than ever, and sometimes you forget he's there. As the days pass, Mom stops smiling while he sits in the kitchen when she's ironing the shirts that aren't permanent press—she's hoping one day that all shirts will be made of permanent press—ice cubes melting in the glass of watery

Pepsi in front of him on the table. He eats supper like he's a ro-bot, one day stabbing his fork into the butter dish and taking a bite, chewing until Mom says, *Lew! Lew! What are you doing!* He spits the yellowish glob onto his plate and looks as if he has just woken up and has to remember who we are.

An uncle is someone who marries a woman who teaches high school French, but that doesn't happen for quite a while because, according to what Mother tells Suzanne, he's very shy. Shy is how *you* are, but you think his shyness is not the same. You think, even, your mother is wrong. But what do you know, you're only a girl, though you are changing, which is something that Uncle Lew is less likely than ever to notice.

When he brings his new wife to meet the family, you're as ex-cited as anyone, but you can't help noticing how Sally looks a lot like Mother, except her hair is blonde while your mother's is brown, and Sally is younger, of course. Yet they both have those sharp features, ice-blue eyes, and overflowing bodies that they cover in flower-print dresses hemmed just above the knee, oddly fine-boned ankles they show off in strappy sandals with little heels.

An uncle is someone who must have happy times like anyone, but the last you see of him before his funeral, he looks as if he hasn't laughed for a long time. He sits in a lawn chair under the maple be-side his wife, Sally in her powder-blue shift. A yellow leaf drifts down onto his lap. You're too old to try to make him laugh by clowning around, so you just smile in case he looks in your direction. Some-where in the neighborhood, someone is burning something, prob-ably a pile of brush, bits of nature that are unnecessary, to be rid of. The harsh smell of the fire doesn't seem to bother anyone. Inside your head you whisper *Uncle Lew, Uncle Lew.*

What you remember later is how he was there and not there, a maple leaf fluttering unnoticed on top of his pants in the acrid breeze that afternoon.

JUNK SHOP PHOTO

THE OLD PHOTO SHOWED unexpected ghost-like images. Who expects phantoms in the film? Some may. Not them. It wasn't in their psychology. Impossible to imagine their psyches as part of the collective unconsciousness. Largely unconscious, their day-to-day perambulation must leave spirit out of things. That supernatural shit? Aunt Dimmy's domain. Out in the countryside. She could look at a hand, hold the limp weight of your wrist, track down something behind your eyes. You didn't want to go there.

Aunt Dimmy's with her tin of currant biscuits, the squawking bird in the cage next to the window, the morning sun slant through the glass onto the woven-rag rug. Aunt Dimmy said not to go with that man, his camera packed up tight, everything he owned in this world on his back. The pointed toes of his dusty boots kicking up stones in the pathway.

He just smiled when you said you couldn't go, that Aunt Dimmy said no; him looking through you with eyes that cut like glass splintering sundown when it touches the china cabinet front. He knew you would follow. He knew you would knock on the soft wooden door of the shack. You would take down your panties, shivering while sweat collected behind your knees and pinpricked your temples.

The photos don't show that. They don't show a girl with the map of her future imprinted in her palms, the blue veins branched in her eyelids. Someone will buy the old photos in a junk shop seventy-some years later and wonder only at the fog-like blurs, some phenomena of mistakes long since eradicated.

THE OSSUARY

S HE FELL INTO SOMETHING with him almost immediately, a spell she decided to call love. Twenty-five years old, she'd thought she'd known love before, and was now happy to be on her own, undiminished, traveling European places she'd never been. At the café in Prague where she stopped for a cup of cocoa, he looked long at her, a look that burned through her. She'd never seen eyes like his, and hasn't since—green with an indigo rim encircling the irises.

Such a moment must mean something. Often it does. October, it was quite warm, and the sky was the sky, polished and infinite. He spoke, questions that seemed genuinely to want answers. And though she'd spoken to no one for many days and her voice seemed at first lost to her, soon they talked easily enough. He was no longer a stranger. She agreed to let him accompany her to the Sedlec Ossuary.

Months ago, she'd read all the literature on the macabre site, about the carpenter who'd been hired in the 1800s to put order to the bones of the forty thousand dead. She thought she was prepared, eager even, for the sight, chandeliers constructed from bones.

The train ride passed quickly, and they arrived at the decaying Kutna Hora station, where, as in Prague, the clerk did not speak English. The aging signage displayed town names bereft of vowels. They set out walking to the ossuary.

Inside, he took her hand. Wordlessly, they traipsed through the chapel while an aura of heat built to enclose their connected hands. Her senses heightened, dizzying her. She shut her eyes against the carefully placed medallions of femurs, ulnae, and skulls. He pulled her outside and kissed her, and she experienced the sensation of sinking deep within herself, as if into an internal chamber where a true part of herself had always waited to welcome her arrival.

Holding hands—their living flesh and bones—nothing had ever felt as natural or as significant. When they made love, she found all those vowels missing from the language. She was who she'd been meant to be.

But life is never only a moment. Through the passing days, she would become other selves as the moments allowed. Yet, she would never forget the one inside who'd been the first to welcome her to herself.

(The man? He'd had a lover he would never leave, and though she despised infidelity, she couldn't despise him. They'd had what they'd had. A time easy to come and easy to go.)

YOUR SPREE IN PARIS

P*ARIS IN THE SPRINGTIME*. Who hasn't heard the words? Going to Paris in the springtime is a kind of cliché to transcend, many understand that—and they transcend it. Some of us understand that it's bound not to be all it's cracked up to be. Decades of dirt and rubbish and tourism and the global economy since the heyday of the ex-pats, Gertrude Stein and her salons. Riots and car burnings in the streets.

But some of us must see it for ourselves, nonetheless.

You never mentioned the City of Lights when we met—Life Painting Seminar I—nor ever talked about it the years since. Yet, evidently, the urge was there.

Today, practically anyone can arrange to go to Paris, if one wants to.

One might be an artist who is not paid nearly well enough for his drudgery—laying out quarterly publications for a nonprofit organization using Photoshop and all the latest programs—and still—secretly—put together the money for the trip, such a necessary validation of his artistic vision and ability. Or one might be an artist like me, who is perhaps less talented, perhaps not in possession of any natural genius, who does not find her graphic design work so utterly useless and unappealing, doesn't once consider a trip to Paris, and certainly doesn't stealthily squirrel away her earnings.

Why not Vienna? I would see Klimt at the Belvedere Palace; I'd pilgrimage to the Attersee to view the villa Klimt rented on a hill close to the lake in Seewalchen. There, I'd walk the hills to find some of the views he painted. He used a telescope to create those cropped looks, the foreshortened depth in his landscapes painted on a square format, the square being the perfect proportion to his Secessionist mind. I would like to be in the presence of the dazzling poplar paintings, the natural palettes of masterful grays, the blockish tree-sky-pocket hat trick in *Tall Poplars I.* Don't disbelieve that Klimt calls to me, that philanderer who fathered at least fourteen illegitimate children, who said that all art is erotic—who said, "Whoever wants to know something about me, as an artist, which alone is significant, they should look attentively at my pictures and there seek to recognize what I am and what I want." He was, at least, honest.

You are probably at the Place des Vosges today, this Wednesday here (Thursday there) being the first day of your spree. Like every visitor, you would begin here—I now see you for who you are—at the oldest and most beautiful square. In my office, I scour photos on the Internet. This image shows arcades, arch after arch lining the sidewalk that runs the length of the four connected buildings that form the square. Place des Vosges—what is "Vosges"? I learn the term is nothing more or less than the name of mountains in the background.

In the center of the square, the very green rolling lawn contains fountains and statuary, but the main surprise is the people spread over the grass—so many people. Not your ideal. You've always made a point of how you are a loner, that's your preference. Klimt lived a simple, cloistered life, in which he avoided other artists and café society. And yet. Many, many children. His subject the female body.

Down the hall from my office, Brenda pauses at Daniel's office, replies to something he's said. She's en route to ask me how the watershed poster is coming; it needs to go to the printers Friday, and as yet I've given her nothing to approve. I click out of the browser and pull the program back up on my screen even though it's my lunch break and there's certainly nothing wrong with looking at images of Paris on my own time. Though I can't hear Brenda's words to my office mate, her tone sounds strained.

I zoom in on the last frame of the poster, where the trouble is. The text is poorly executed—you have to strain to read the labels. But this is because of the muddy brown color of the creek in the background, which really can't be changed this late in the game. "Change it," Brenda says.

I jump, and that makes me angry. "That will mean changing the tone," I begin.

"Which means, yes, altering the contrast up there in frame one, the trees, the rest." She points out the edits. Her voice trails off reflectively, and I'm pretty sure what she's going to say next. "Too busy. There's too much—"

"I know," I interrupt her. "I know, I know, I know." As if repeating the words will do anything.

"How can I help?" she asks simply, to her credit.

The screen blurs as tears well up. I tilt my head down, hair falling forward on each side of my face, and struggle for control. "It will be ready by end of business today," I manage.

Brenda goes on her way, carrying the wrong idea with her. I don't feel sorry for myself for having to do the work. I feel sorry for myself that I'm grateful for having something I have to do.

"Aleita." I think I hear you saying my name but there's no one in the bed but me. Yet on that liminal precipice between sleep and wakefulness, the empty space doesn't first convince me: if I listen hard, you might speak again. Nothing in the hot August night but a far-off troupe of restless insects. Ambient light filters through the open windows, sieved by the craggy tree limbs, still and unmoving. It takes a long time for my heart to stop thumping. In the morning when I wake, nightgown soaked, propped up against the headboard, my neck stiff and aching, I'm amazed to have fallen back to sleep.

"Aleita Bombita." You said that to me a hundred years ago.

"Bert Flirt," I returned.

"Me? I'm no flirt," you said. You shook your head, offering a crooked smile. "I can't flirt," you said. "But for you"—you hooked my arm through yours, and I thought what an odd, old-fashioned thing to do, but I was charmed, it looked good on you— "maybe I could learn."

Arm in arm we left the coffee shop and we walked up King Street, up Marion, up Charles, up Buren. All those timeworn buildings, bracketed cornices, cupolas, tower-of-the-winds columns, pedimented pavilions on gabled rooftops. Two hours later, we were still walking the Savannah streets. We made what we wanted ours, claiming it with our newly appreciative gaze. Falling in love. Cracks in the sidewalks gathered the city's debris in microcosmic patterns. If one could only become small enough to see. Magnificence could be revealed. We agreed on that then, that it was all about revealing what already existed, seeing in a new way.

A bus came along and we took it back to campus, and we must have been that couple, so sickeningly wrapped up in one another to the exclusion of anything or anyone else. Framed in the bus window, our faces, yellowed in the light, were unlikely to have been beacons to pedestrians we passed, though we may have had a sense of ourselves as such, of that being who we were.

"It's one thing to take a sudden trip when you've saved up all the money; it's quite another when you max out a credit card to do it. Without word one. A sneak."

We were fighting and I hated the words that came out of my mouth. But I couldn't go back on them either. Not that you were asking me to. Not that you were acting like I'd said anything surprising at all. It was as if you'd made up your mind that I was a certain way and you were another, and whatever I would say, whatever I did say, only proved you right.

You looked out the open living room window. A girl walked by with her fat dog on a leash. She glanced over, perhaps she had heard me; I saw her catch your eye and you didn't exactly smile—your mouth did not move but it softened, your whole face softened, and I was jealous. I wanted the softening for me. I had the credit card bill in my hand, and I threw it at you. I left the room, ashamed. I didn't want to be the kind of woman who threw things. But evidently I was. I cried, pushing my face into the pillow on the bed. You didn't come into the room. I was glad of that: I didn't want to be the kind of woman who ran off and cried into her pillow.

And I was also sad and wounded. You had been saving money for this—how long! That revelation, and the fact that you couldn't wait to save anymore but had charged the rest of it, your ticket, made me understand not only that you were going, but also how desperate you were to go. Without me. That was what most upset and frightened me: that you did not want me to go with you.

I don't have to go to Paris to get some creative work done. I am determined to paint while you are gone. The days pass, and who can tell how long this spree of yours will last, no word from you. I've gone into the studio two different nights after work, and how dusty, how disordered! I've seen that I will have to spend most of the weekend cleaning in order to even begin.

I plan to tell you when we talk that I rather resent having to be the one left with this mess, which will take up all my creative time tonight. By saying so, you will know that I'm serious again about my painting.

I will not be one of those women who, when you call, refuses to voice my complaints out of some misguided fear of pushing you further away. You *are* away. You were not pushed. You took yourself there.

I gather some rags and the dustpan and start on my side of the studio. Stacks of old newsprint. Abandoned sketches. Pencils with teeth marks notching their bodies. I toss it all. Really, I don't think I'll do anything with your side of the room; why should I? If I did, obviously I would have to tell you that I've cleaned your side—it's not I who withholds information—and I'm not going to be that woman, having cleaned up your dirty studio, telling you on the phone from the other side of the world as if to entice you back. As if I should like a pat on the head, give the good dog a bone.

Perhaps I'll say nothing at all about the studio or about my creative work, which will surely be underway by the time you call, not tonight. Some other night. When you are finished with your spree. How much you disliked me calling it that, your jaw tightening at the word. But that's not why you don't call me. That's not why you stay away.

The dustpan clatters to the floor, loosing the collected debris. It's quite beautiful, this pattern of grit and grime scattered over the old floorboards. I see that, clear-eyed. I begin to photograph it. And at the opening of my first show, someone will ask that usual question about how I got started taking pictures, and I'll think of this night, of you, a blurry image in my mind's eye that won't come true.

MY FATHER AND HIS
BEAUTIFUL SLIM BRUNETTES

MY OWN WORDS WOKE me up the way it sometimes happens. Manny sat on the edge of the bed, shaving cream stripped away in swaths on his left cheek, razor still in hand. The water trickled into the sink basin and the fluorescent light glowed miserably over the mirror. I turned away toward the windows. Between the crack in the motel's heavy drapes, the day shone bright.

"Active night," Manny said. The mattress jounced when he stood and returned to shaving. "It sounded like your dad had a harem or something."

I wasn't sure I understood what he said; his words were garbled from the way he stretched the skin over his face to hold it taut. I rolled over, and his eyes in the mirror met mine before flicking back to his own face, watching the razor move close to his mouth. Damp hair clung to his nape, a towel wrapped around his beautiful torso. He adjusted the water, rinsed the razor, and finished.

"Do you remember your dream?" He sat on the bed again, all clean soapy smell. I shook my head. Manny repeated what I'd evidently said in my sleep, "My father and his slim beautiful brunettes." His hands roamed his knees, fingers absentmindedly tracing the kneecaps, his eyes taking on that look of concentration fixed somewhere distant, ephemeral.

"You get the idea of a ring of nymphets frolicking atop a round hill," he said. "There's moonlight, deliciously licking their bodies white against a midnight-blue backdrop." His hands massaged the flesh above the kneecaps—his knees always gave him trouble, stiff and sore, and that worried him, went against his image. "Picture mermaids, swimmy seductive scallops, long hair languidly flowing."

"Sirens singing," I said.

Female country singers, guitar straps looped over pale, shapely shoulders, blossoms of pink mouths crooning into microphones tucked into elegant, lissome fingers—my father in a trance helpless before their images on the TV screen, the volume blaring.

Manny licked his forefinger and took it to my eyebrow, straightening the wildness of my thick brows. I said, "You don't see my mother in her wedding dress, fists of anxiety nesting, hidden, among the white-netted folds."

"No, you don't." He shook his head, working on the other eyebrow.

Manny and I sat quiet and still for a bit, thoughts following thoughts. He gave me a tentative smile. I'd always been defenseless before that smile. On stage, when I hit certain notes, he'd catch my eye, turn that smile on me while he played some kind of razzle-dazzle on his guitar.

I returned the smile, and we spent some last motel time together in one another's arms before I prodded him into going out to load the band equipment on the truck with the other guys.

"It is going to get hot pretty soon," he agreed.

In the hush of the room after, I felt drowsy, my bones heavy on the mattress. My eyes wouldn't stay open. Images from the biography series I'd watched each night on TV while Manny was out calling his wife swam in my mind's eye—the female country singers swathed in fluid, sequined gowns cinched at their waists. Slim hips undulating like mermaids during those last strained moments on land before they had to go home. Beauties with that whining pain in their voices, seemingly as natural as silvery bubbles trailing in the mermaids' wakes. Watching the footage, I'd seen how it could have seemed to my father that they sang those notes just for him, how that feeling grew to overwhelm him. It didn't seem possible that there could be anyone else more full of yearning, longing, and needing than he.

My father was my James Dean before I knew who James Dean was and why he was cool. He carried his Lucky Strikes in his white T-shirt sleeves rolled up over his bicep, his thick hair dark as the night we sliced through. Eight years old, I hung on behind on his motorcycle, holding my eager arms around his solid middle loosely, careful not to cling. Once after we'd gotten home and he parked, when I scrambled down from the seat, sneakers crunching into the gravel driveway, he turned around, surprised, and said he'd forgotten I was there. We took curves and corners fast, the bike dipping sideways, dangerously close to the road.

My hair was dark like his but Mother clipped it short, my bangs like the fringe of an eyelash. I was light; Mother, in the kitchen washing supper dishes while we rode, weighed close to two hundred pounds. My father didn't like being weighed down. He liked speed in the night and its freedom enough to pay. I was the fee, stuck like a postage stamp on the envelope delivering him.

My father liked my high school girlfriend Cathy Miller. Though often I was grounded—I was hopeless, wild, bad, defiant—with Cathy by my side, I could do anything, go anywhere. She took ballet lessons, played the piano, smiled a lot. She looked like Loretta Lynn. Cathy didn't like the things I did, most of which she didn't know about. I don't know whether she liked *me* all that much. But I stuck to her, my alibi. Instead of spending the night at Cathy's, I was in the boys' dorm of the nearby college with Professor Miller's students—her father taught history—singing at the raucous parties while Cathy was home in bed, tired after ballet practice or studying for a civics test.

When Cathy came to my house, my father, trying for a hobby that would keep him home, made fudge. He used marshmallows and nuts, his special ingredients. He gave Cathy the wooden spoon to lick clean. He liked to watch her lick the spoon and liked how, skimming her long, brunette hair back over her perfect shoulders, she said, "Mmm."

Once Cathy's mother, a busy businesswoman, picked Cathy up from my house to go shopping. "Come along," she said. Brisk, no-nonsense, she led us into Ausdale's where she bought two summer dress suits, and then in the junior's department a bikini for Cathy. The crocheted bathing suit was orange and yellow. In the dressing room, Cathy looked sensational: slim, long-legged, arms all sinewy, sculpted with grace.

She made me try it on. I suppose she needed to fulfill some sense of equanimity between us. After some coaxing I did, to please her; I stood looking in the full-length mirror, feeling her looking, hearing the surprise and admiration in her voice. "It looks better on you! Perfect, you're perfect!" I knew, at that moment, that were my father to see, he would think it a lie. Illusion. And I knew there would never be another moment I would see myself as a slender, beautiful brown-haired girl and hear *you're perfect!*

"Not my style," I told her.

Cathy Miller is probably still slender and shapely, preparing perhaps to become the mother of daughters with long dark hair, all career and schools, clubs and activities, a cozy breakfast nook, a husband who admires her from across the room at social gatherings. Her years since high school haven't been a roller coaster, a series of apartments in skyscraper cities with planters of compacted arid soil and desiccated poinsettias, stage clothing left in suitcases.

My father and his beautiful, slim brunettes.

Elaine, who was married to the son of my father's boss. Benny was supposed to apprentice under my father to learn the business that he would take over. But Benny did not learn how to measure, cut, hammer, install kitchen cabinetry. In the office, he talked on the telephone to Elaine, who'd been happy and popular in high school just weeks before. A classic romance soured by pregnancy. Elaine finished her senior year privately tutored at home. She took lunch to Benny in the shop, and soon her bags included home-baked goodies for my father, too.

My mother said nothing when my father reported what Elaine had brought to the shop that day. Later on, my parents socialized with Elaine and Benny, after the couple had a second child and a third on the way, going to their house to play cards, taking peanuts and potato chips that they bickered about, the chips in all the different varieties, flavors, brands, and textures good for long squabbles. I kept out of the way, stayed up in my bedroom until after they'd gone, and emerged downstairs into a silence echoing with its own fullness. The pleasure of sprawling on the living room floor alone reading, undisturbed. Not needing to go anywhere. Of course it didn't last. The card parties ended and a siege of fights began, *Elaine* reverberating from the instruments of their mouths.

Elaine and Benny went out, and I babysat. Daniel and Rachel were good little kids. They watched TV and ate ice cream, brushed their teeth—I had to help Rachel, who wasn't yet two—and went to bed without complaint. Daniel was fair and blond, pale and thin, so quiet he seemed not of this world. Asleep in his bed, he didn't seem to use any air. I positioned my face close to his to make sure he breathed.

Rachel had large, interested brown eyes and dark brown hair, hair like mine, unsmooth and wild. She was beautiful, she would always be. Once I brought with me a photo of myself as a tot and held the picture next to Rachel's face. She blinked her eyes like she was winking at me and reached for the photo. When I gave it over, she pressed it to her mouth. I watched her fall asleep in her crib. She sang to herself, her baby voice clear, the photo close to her mouth. When I knew she was sleeping, I untangled the snapshot from her fingers and worked it under her mattress.

My hair was not becoming, my parents said, Mother sometimes pulling it for emphasis. They didn't know what they were talking about. I'd seen pictures of Janis Joplin, and, though no one said she was pretty, she had presence, and no one could deny her that voice. Out of the house, I junked myself up like Janis, working feathers and beads into my hair. I stacked rings on my fingers and bangles up my arms, roped chains around my hips and my neck; I wore anklets with tiny jangling bells. Boys admired me, bell-bottoms riding low, singing at their parties, letting my voice sound their yearnings, the way that Janis would have done it.

At home, I sang in our cavernous bathroom, the acoustics making me shiver, and one day my brother, who had his own problems, bounded up the stairs to hit me, thinking I was playing his album he'd forbidden me to touch. I smirked, admiring my smirk in the mirror—ironic and knowing and sophisticated. "Groovy, man," I whispered-growled like I'd heard Janis say, followed with her raspy laugh on the *Dick Cavett Show*. I laughed, and he punched my arm.

He was ill-tempered because my father had his car again. My father drove his beautiful brunette in Mark's red Mustang because he liked speed in the night and it was past motorcycle season—and no doubt he felt what was his son's was his. Mark was through with it, he said, done with cleaning my father's pecker tracks from the back-seat. Sickening phrase, "pecker tracks." I could have vomited. Mark smiled. "Come on, let's walk uptown," he said.

I preferred going uptown by myself; Mark was critical of every boy. But when my father had his car, I felt sorry for him since he couldn't pick up girls. The thing he liked besides his car was girls. Girls, and his hair. Mark's smooth, glossy dark hair rained down his back—hair for which my father called him a girl, had once held him down, trying to cold-cock him so he could shear him. I went uptown with Mark, deprived of his girls.

Mark always wanted to talk about our father and his brunette. Mark described the things my father did with her in the backseat of the Mustang parked on the edge of town by the lake. "We ought to go there, surprise them in the fogged-over windows," he said. Anger crammed into his voice and made it jagged, a voice hard to hear. He drew fiercely on cigarettes, chain smoking his way uptown, the red tips quick furious dots in the dark. Those were my cigarettes he sucked down, but it wasn't worth mentioning.

We reached the park where boys gathered around the bronze statue, a memorial to the veterans of World War I. Maybe it was World War II, but the important thing was that the immense cast soldiers were good for hiding behind. You held yourself tight and compact behind their impervious forms, or squeezed beside them, in front of them—any direction opposite of the slow-stalking police cruiser that circled the park.

While I smoked with the boys, I assessed their behavior, what they said, how they looked when they said what they said, evaluating and deciding on the one I'd pick. Rarely were other girls there. Some-times, someone else's girlfriend. Mark and some of the guys would get stoned, talking about where to go get girls, about getting up the balls to steal somebody's parents' car—whose? How?

I don't know how, once they left, they got girls. Maybe other towns, dances, skating rinks. Mark slept in late the following mornings and appeared in the kitchen around noon, smiling and happy.

Me and my boy hung around the statue making out, or went back to his house if his parents weren't home or were the kind who stayed in their chairs in front of the TV when we went downstairs into the den or upstairs to the attic, or into the boy's bedroom, if it was that kind of house. Rich assholes, Mark called the boys from that kind of house.

So what? That was best. Comfort, no concrete, a bed, no cold. You could remove clothes; there were blankets. Music. The stereo's luminous green dial in the dark. A black light was nice.

Fair or not, I went first for boys coming from a house like that. I mean, any boy could eventually get that we lived in nowheresville, but these boys already knew a world was out there. It was pictured on the album covers scattered in their rooms. They had the evidence of a world where there was Janis. A world where girls longed like her, and went where they wanted to go.

Then Mark's beautiful slim brunette got pregnant. My father kicked him out for a while, long enough for Mark to drop out of school and start working at the cannery. When the hubbub died down, the girl, now Mark's wife, came to live in our house, too, and my father found that even with her swollen abdomen she was a beauty, smiled a hell of a lot like June Carter Cash. He and Debby got along pretty well.

Debby went into my bedroom, stole my underpants, ruined them stretching the elastic over her stomach; she read my boys' notes and lied about it. I tried to feel sympathetic: the best thing that had ever happened to her was Mark. I felt sorry for her for what was going to be her life.

But it grew to be too much. Debby carrying cups of coffee, chocolate chip cookies arranged in a circle on the plate to my father where he reclined in his chair watching TV. Him smiling at her. Him out of the blue telling me that my hips were beginning to roll when I walked, and I'd better watch myself or I'd wind up looking like my mother.

Seventeen is not too young to be on your own. If you have something, like a voice. And luck.

My favorite gigs were weeklong bookings at hotels. Less time on the road in the beast of a truck, tired and bored, physically aching, my lumbar complaining from the hard seats. Setting up and tearing down only once in a week. Minimal sound checks each night. I woke up in the same bed with no rush to get anywhere. I took baths, ate regularly.

Manny fretted about these hotel house-band gigs, about the lack of exposure. He perched on the bed, plucking at his guitar and fussing. I always wished he'd shut up, though I knew he was right. Guilt tainted my contentment. It had taken years to get this far, to enjoy this level of comfort, and that was mostly to Manny's credit, his drive. He deserved loyalty.

Ironic that we were at a Ramada Inn in Buffalo when the label asked to sign us.

It wasn't immediately clear who they were, two bland guys with thinning hair and the builds of middle-aged men who believed playing golf once a week kept them in decent shape. Dressed in khakis and loafers, they ordered expensive drinks. If there was any betrayal of their identities, it was in the intensity with which they watched us play. But then, there were always those kinds of guys—they often stood right at the lip of the stage—mourning lost chances at being rock stars.

We were playing our hearts out, different from the way we usually treated a Tuesday night, which was more like practice, oblivious

to the scattering of happenstance listeners and the handful of drink-
ers at the bar, no one dancing.

It was a good contract; in our room, Manny read it over briefly.
He'd studied all this, knew everything there was to know—we'd never needed a manager, he was that good at the business side, though
we'd all agreed when we reached this point we'd hire someone to take
over. We all waited, edgy, barely containing our excitement while he
went through the pages, nodding, a huge smile spreading over his
face as he flipped over the last page. "It's all here," he said. "All really,
really fucking good."

We returned to the bar with the mocked-up contract, which
Manny pronounced we'd be signing. A time was set on Friday morning when we'd bring our lawyer—Manny had had someone in mind
forever—and meet with the execs and their lawyers at label head-
quarters in NYC. It was going to happen. Manny's eyes were blood-
shot, stratified with excitement and pride, and like the other guys',
lit with disbelief everyone pretended wasn't that.

Hotel staff brought trays of drinks, shots, and beers, and a specta-
cle of food: omelets, specialty sausages, mangoes, kiwis, other nameless exotic fruits, sad caviar. Bottles of champagne popped. We were
used to eating after shows that ran to the wee early hours, after all the
energy we expended on stage and the added labor of tearing down
and loading up of equipment on single-date gigs, but this was a feast.
A huge slab of roasted pig with glazed pineapple rings appeared—a
disgusting sight, really, but the guys dug in.

One of the agents snapped pictures, and the hotel management,
anxiously laughing, posed as they served us. I could imagine the stories they were forming—conjured pieces already glimmered in their
eyes—for telling at home that night. They, too, had produced cam-
eras. Manny and I were careful not to locate ourselves near one another. We'd always been prudent; we'd seen no reason to complicate

our lives, especially Manny's. He did love his wife, and I knew Sheila only a very little but enough to understand why.

The agent with the camera was swarthy dark, soft, hair thinning at the temples. He tried to catch my eye while he drank down shots of J.D. Ours wasn't a drinking band, not really. But we'd have eight weeks off before going into the studio, and the champagne went down easy. Sure, Manny would drive us to practice, practice, practice, but we'd be home. With family, friends, Manny's wife, the other guys' girlfriends— they were all high on that. I could find myself a new apartment, sunny and spacious, where at least the stillness sparkled.

Manny returned to the room, out of breath. They'd loaded the truck in record time. He threw his things into his bag, though he tried not to look as if he was in a hurry. "Come on, darling, let's get on the road." He must have gone into the bathroom six times, swinging the door wide open and checking the back to make sure nothing had been left hanging on the hook. When he swept open the shower curtains, I said, "You know, you can always buy new shampoo. You can afford it now."

Manny collapsed onto the bed beside me. His sweat reeked of whiskey. He wrapped himself around me, his shoes heavy on top of the covers. One thunked painfully onto my ankle. I shifted us around until we were the most comfortable I was going to be, and I squeezed him. Manny deserved it, this feeling that he was on top, everything peaking. He'd worked hard, fretted, herded, pushed, championed. Sometimes, exasperated, the guys called him Dad.

I felt in his body how he was really zinging, so ready for going. I gave him some more solid squeezes. "Oh, honey," he said, getting it then, that I wasn't going to ride back with them in the truck.

I held him hard. My mouth registered his neck's salty sting. His long fingers combed through my hair, taking the time while I felt his whole body wanting to be gone, to be elsewhere. The effort it took for him to remain. "She's going to be really proud, Manny, really proud and excited. You have to get going, go tell her."

He pulled back and lifted his head at my words, and he gave me his shy-happy smile, one I knew well. I could have told him right then that it was over, and some part of me wanted to, the part that obsessively held the image of my dark empty room up in my mind's eye. But I was proud that I was a woman who shunned drama. Who didn't need to be the center of attention in anyone's life. I got all the attention I needed up there on the stage. A shadow crossed Manny's face as if he knew my thoughts. We'd always been able to read each other—we'd written songs together. "Be careful on the road," I said.

The cue he'd been waiting for. He stood and retied a shoe, and made sure I had enough money, taking bills out of his wallet. After NYC, this would never happen again, I thought, a complex surge of emotion rattling me.

The door shut loud, and I clamped the pillow over my head. Images of Manny and Sheila post-coital bombarded me; they'd be dreaming their new house, their new baby, which Sheila had been patiently waiting for. The images flooded in, and something else. The pillow became soaked, my face wet with tears.

I slept maybe twenty hours or more. Arose in a new day, the past already behind me. I put my stuff together quickly, leaving a lot of stuff. I'd be forced to celebrate the luxury of buying new things.

The car rental place offered coffee, and I poured a large cup to go. Within a few miles, I pulled into a gas station with a convenience store, where I cruised the aisles looking for something palatable. I grabbed a package of animal crackers and refilled my coffee. I decided to top off the gas while I was there, and then felt idiotic when, returning to the register to pay, the cashier raised his eyebrows and said, "A dollar seventeen."

Traffic was light on the highway. I refused to play music. The drive needed to stretch out, to feel like the pilgrimage it was.

But it wasn't a hundred miles before I arrived, and I hadn't even finished drinking the refill. My father answered the door. His musculature had softened with age, and he wore silver-rimmed glasses. I experienced a tiny breathless charge at the grasp of how long it'd been.

Silence first, like I knew there'd be. No astonishment in him, and I realized then that earlier, when I'd been imagining his surprise, I'd forgotten how he was. While he studied me standing in the doorway, I comprehended that he was, after all, surprised somewhere inside himself—that was why it was taking him so long to ask me inside.

Then I saw the truth of how it was. He didn't have to ask me in; he might not. His hand wormed around in his shirt pocket, digging into the cigarette pack there and searching the slight space for a light.

I tried to think of something to say, an ending, so that I could head out, go home, with ease. When he spoke, he startled me, and I hated that I jumped.

"I expect you think that I'll comment on your hair"—it was just growing back in, peach fuzz, bleached white—"you probably thought that I'd say something about it, but I won't."

He opened the door for me and moved in the direction of the den.

I slipped into the kitchen. My mother, round-shouldered, turned from where she stood at the sink rinsing a cup. Her eyes went over me, shocked at my bony frame, my ninety-something pounds. I'd forgotten everything about me until then, when my parents made it visible in their faces. She turned the faucet off so hard that the pipes underneath the sink clunked. "Welcome back," she said, her voice sheltering bitterness. I don't think she looked at me again.

I followed her to the den. She walked slowly now. My dad sat in his recliner, eyes averted, and Mark's face clenched at the sight of me. He'd cry except that he was too angry. I'd gotten away. "Long time no see," he said. He returned his attention to his son, maybe seven or eight, who sat not at all comfortably in his father's lap, holding an old storybook. I gathered that the kid had been charged with reading aloud. My entrance had given him a reprieve, but now the pressure was back on.

The TV volume hid some of his soft mewing protests.

Mark threatened the boy with a father voice he'd learned, so the kid began in a small voice. His lonely sound quivered; you wondered what he heard of himself.

But there wasn't time for that because Mark said, and Mother said, "I can't hear you!"

"We can't," Mother repeated.

The little boy sucked in his breath and started over.

Mark interrupted. "Your aunt can't hear you."

Not once did my father lower the volume on the TV.

The boy again collected himself. His fingers worried the hem of his jeans, his face pale.

I took that small pause. I told the kid that I'd heard him loud and clear, and then, I told him that to tell the truth, I didn't want to hear the story. "Everyone knows the story."

His solemn blinking like Rachel's. Me zipping up my jacket. Everyone in the den like just another audience who happened to be in a place where I also happened to be. The remote on the arm of my father's chair like some venerable icon, his power ring. I felt nutty laughter cracking up inside me. I took his little plastic box of sad control from him. Shaking, I was shaking with wanting so much to say some one right thing, the exact words. I wanted words that would ring so true that they'd be undeniable for everyone.

My mother would be forced to admit *Oh, how foolish we've been!* Everyone would begin talking at once, and everything would end in agreement, that they—we—could leave it all in the past.

The nerves inside my brain felt scoured by sandpaper. I pressed my thumb down, sending up the TV volume.

What I remember about leaving the den was seeing in my peripheral vision something new and raw on the little boy's face that, later, as I recalled it, as I often did, I liked to think was a spark of an idea about how he could be.

POND WATER

INSIDE, BY THE BACK door, a plastic bucket of cold water holds two nishikigoi. Their shadows flicker across the pink plastic and make her think of the rotating paper lamp in her childhood nursery. She never realized how much the red bucket has faded.

Because of the superiority of her pond, architectured for their well-being, her koi have been properly finished, meaning they've reached their highest potential, and certainly must win a prize at the Koi Club judging. She sits inside the vestibule on the cool slate floor across from the bucket while the sun moves west in the sky. The fish appear to hang suspended in the water.

As per the experts' advice, they haven't been fed for five days. Perhaps their bodies have begun to cannibalize themselves. She herself can't feel her own shrunken stomach; the ache of hunger dissipated on the third day.

It grows late and she can't so much see the pink bucket as remember where it rests in the dark. She feels her way on hands and knees across the cold slate, and kneeling beside the bucket reaches inside the water to take Albert, the larger of the pair, into her hand. He lets her. She brings the fish to her mouth. He remains passive in her palm. She could eat him up, she could. She returns him to the water, its pH now spoiled: it's taken only a moment.

The handle of the bucket cuts into the flesh of her hand as she travels the moonlit path to the pond, where unceremoniously she dumps the nishikigoi. She remembers something about a fairytale—was it a certain spell?—the nursery lamp splashing shadows over the ceiling. Someone read the story to her, a man whose breath smelled like stagnant water. Something can be ruined in an instant, without care. She turns back toward the ancient house.

❧ THREE ❧

SHE ONLY DABBLED IN MAGIC
TO AMUSE HERSELF

HIS APARTMENT
IN THE CITY

S HE WALKED TO HIS apartment, monotonous building on the hill, the brick façade indistinguishable from the next, where no one bothered to hang colored prayer flags from windows. He would smile when she arrived, the smile a lie.

In that moment she'd wonder who she was, inscrutable to herself, a mystery for some other time, one she might not ever solve. (She was someone's sister. Her sister, who'd always been kind, had left the city long ago.)

She lived life how she could, unable to say no to certain things, proclivities she might list on her deathbed, should someone care to ask. She would never have a child who would take on that role. (Her sister had wanted children and had them, two sullen girls, always in trouble. Her sister, who'd had soft-looking hair caught up in barrettes on either side of her face like swooping dark wings of an enigmatic bird, often looked haunted, dark eyes burning her papery face. The girls, no one asked about anymore. Preservation had its own rules.)

Wiping mist from her face, she stumbled up the crumbling stairs to his apartment, arranging her expression, at the top waiting for him to open the door. Orange shadows welcomed her.

He would smile his thin smile. Time would narrow and blur. The shadows would transform, grow dark, long, sharp. Afterward, she'd rise and walk home, the city surrounding her like a mother, indifferent, unmoved.

OTHER SIDE

"IT'S NOT WHAT YOU think," I say to my sister, but she's quiet, looking out the kitchen window at the globe of light, her fingers itchy for a cigarette. A nurse who smokes, but I understand. That light out the window, the soft glow pulsating. Strobes of lavender, green, yellow slant over my sister's cheeks. They pick up a glitter slithering from under one eye. The tear trails down to hang from her jaw.

We had that time together when we were children: we dug something up from the dirt in the backyard; she, the older, had a dingy soup spoon found somewhere, I a stick that kept breaking, but we rooted it out, the browned bone of the wild creature. "Part of a leg," she said. She was always sad about her own legs, thought them too thick and went on starvation diets until her glossy hair dulled and began falling out. I should have told her then, it's not what you think. I knew that a svelte figure would never bring her the love she craved.

Here is this globe of light, just the other side of the glass, and the glass, it opens. Her pale fingers reach for the window, her thin hair pasted to her head. The globe kicks up a wind. The colors of light broaden, a waterfall, waves that transmorph to stairs. It seems to take no effort at all when she climbs through, passing over the windowsill as if it were just another headline in the newspaper about some so-called human interest story. When she looks back before ascending, that tear releases from her jaw, and she spirals higher to an unseen destination. I want to think I'll find the tear later, fossilized, a gem in the dirt for excavation.

WHERE ARE YOU GOING, SISTER?

CATALOG OF COGNITIVE QUIRKS. She has been compiling it since they first cohabitated. Nights, going down to the basement after he's asleep, the heavy snores she hears all the way down the stairs, muffled only when she closes the cellar door. Behind the workshop, a tiny room like a closet she lights with a glass-walled lantern containing a pine-scented candle. It's for the ceremony, and because it smells like Christmas. A present she gives herself.

A rough-hewn shelf keeps the dated ledgers. On the lined pages, she checks off the traits he's exhibited that day. Beginning sentences with the word *now*. A subtle duck of the head after he drinks. The excited way he stamps his feet when she sweeps the kitchen floor. The last quirk isn't real. It isn't really even of the mind.

Through the chinks in the wall, cold air seeps in. Some creature is nearby, silent in the shadows. Where are you going, sister? it thinks, sending her the thought that makes her aware of a longing. The nameless yearning. Pioneers have always acted on those cravings. Ruts gouged in the pathways like grooves in the brain.

A PAIR OF SISTERS

Early in the late summer morning, the older sister starts up the old tractor. The commotion will prise up the younger sister, who lies on her back just over the knoll watching clouds. Sure enough, the top of the younger sister's red ball cap appears as she ascends the hill. Her face grows clearer so that the older sister can see the quizzical expression torquing her severe features.

"What is it?" the younger sister hollers when she is near enough to be heard over the din of the engine.

"The old gal still runs," the older sister says, bringing her fist down on the steering wheel.

The air reeks of diesel. The older sister cuts the engine and a blister of caws erupts in the silence. The wedge of crows lifts from the bare-limbed apple tree. They have other places. The younger sister watches their black wings disappear, tiny dots that vanish in the sere stratosphere. They might almost have been imagined.

The two sisters must share a bedroom in the little white house. From the road, you can tell the squat clapboard can't contain much more than a kitchen and a sitting room. Since 1955, the house has had a bathroom, a boxy windowless attachment stuck to the rear of the house, supported by concrete pillars, sagging.

This morning the sisters are already finishing up breakfast in the kitchen, in the northern side of the house, where the shadows lie long this early in the day. As always, both are unrested and miserable. The two sisters sleep in the same twin beds they always have. The older sister's feet extend to the foot of the bed. Were she a bit taller, her heels would hang over. She sleeps on her back, which annoys the younger sister to no end. She is sure if the older sister would have the consideration to turn on her side, as the younger sister has requested so many times, the older sister's snoring would stop.

The older sister will not do it. She does not have the courtesy. Consequently, the younger sister, who lies considerately on her side, remains awake long into the night and worries about the clouds of broken capillary veins that have begun forming on her feet.

Deep veins crack the dry earth surrounding the clapboard house. The grassy hill, where the younger sister likes to rest and watch the sky, has lost its lush verdure.

The older sister expects rain any day now. Each evening after dinner, she opens her lawn chair near the window in the kitchen, where the younger sister, cleaning up the supper dishes, can see her through the glass above the sink as she rinses the forks. The older sister sits with her cup of muddy coffee, watching the horizon, a look of stubborn insistence on her creased face.

The younger sister is a cloud watcher. She knows no rain is coming. Clouds will continue to gather, to coagulate, to purple. Other things will happen. Maybe a fire. But no rain.

She places her palm, wet with dishwater, on the window glass. The older sister stares at something unseeable in the distance.

UNDER THE ACCUMULATING SUNLIGHT

THE CAKE IS IN the garden, atop the wrought-iron table. Waiting for a lover, an admirer, a friend, anyone other then the squirrel—naughty, naughty squirrel who took a bite out of the woman's beautiful tomato, the first ripened fruit on the vine, a ruby-red valentine in the sun. How disappointed that woman is going to be when she comes out of the house to water the tomato plant. The cake can feel the rosettes in its corners melting, not exactly in sorrow, but in affinity. Under the accumulating sunlight, the cake's sweetness is turning. The squirrel has leapt to the roof, perches on the rain gutter and scolds, for no reason, quieting only when the sugary scent carries to him on the breeze. The cake doesn't want this story of consciousness without agency. The squirrel, eyeing the pink frosting, just wants what it wants.

GILDED CAGE

SHE WAS BELIEVED TO be a witch because of her hunched back. She clothed herself in brown, a thick woven dress even in summer, topped with a heavy brown wool cape in the winter. Substantial brown shoes that could only be called "brogues" tied with aged, fraying shoelaces. Like many, she'd learned to tie her shoes by the time she entered kindergarten. In the kindergarten classroom were mock wooden shoes with white laces that some children had to practice with, less fortunate children who'd never had anyone show them how. There is always a range of abilities, which involve the innate and the circumstance. Today some parents prefer Velcro for their children's shoes, perhaps the same people who don't mind that handwriting is no longer a subject taught in school.

She was believed to be a witch because she was alone and no one had ever been inside her cottage at the edge of the forest and no one knew what she did there. No one imagined that on the other side of the wavy glass panes of the windows, she lived as many do, sometimes by rote and sometimes present to her moments. It's not easy to be present. There is a part of the mind, some may say the larger part, that allows a person to go day to day taking care of living in its basic sense: hunting and gathering and eating and shitting and bathing and sleeping. Some people watch television. Some people listen to music. Some people read. Solve puzzles. One is supposed to have something that one enjoys doing, that makes life worth living. One is supposed to have connections to others; at the very least, a pet.

If anyone had pressed a face to her window, they would have heard the canaries singing in their gilded cage in the living room near the hearth. When the fire was lit, the light of its flames struck the ribs of the cage, and the birds sang, sang. O from the time she was a little girl she'd always loved birdsong, and her father had called her Birdie. Come here, little Birdie, and let me dandle you on my knee! And she went willingly. He was a rough man, many thought, but his large hand was gentle on her waist, and while she rode his thigh like a sure horse galloping down the meadowsides of the green hills, she chirped prettily, notes warmed and bubbled in her throat, and it was a time of being present to herself then, but to think of now, the opposite.

No one knows where we go. Behind the cottage, there are ancient tombstones, markers broken, unmarked with names. They have been there as long as she has been on this earth, wearing her dark clothing, a cape that collects the falling snow, flakes melting from the heat of her back—a back that was always hunched with scoliosis, her spine with its sideways C-shaped curve, the degree of the curve unstable and increasing with the years she gathers. No one had known that small curve existed until the dressmaker who'd hand-sewn her wedding gown saw that one side of the white satin skirt hung lower than the other. Poor misshapen Birdie, she thought, and said nothing, making only the necessary adjustments to the dress so that no one noticed—and indeed, while Birdie waited and waited at the altar for the man who did not come, the hand-beaded gown dazzled while the bride-to-have-been lost her radiance.

This was many years ago. No one knows what became of that man. The father with his withering horse leg never mentioned the day of the jilting to his daughter, not after that night when they sat before the fire drinking whiskey while she used his penknife to hack the glass beads from her skirt, all that she could reach with ease. The beads are in that little sarcophagus of a wooden box on the mantel, someone having swept them up early the next morning and deposited them there. Who had done that? It must have been the woman from the village whom the father had hired to come in once a week to tend to household needs. He hadn't believed in making his daughter a servant.

Gillian had been that woman's name, a sweet-natured person with a lantern jaw, who brought homemade bread and jams to the cottage. How the father had loved those treats and her kindness, and how Gillian had loved the father and Birdie; she could see Birdie's curve growing over time and knew that the young woman would face some pain in her later years, her trunk out of balance, muscles twisted, organs wrung. So perhaps death is sparing in some ways, that a person goes from the earth saved from seeing certain painful developments.

If Birdie were a witch, she would cast spells that would take care of her canaries, for when she is gone it will mean their death too. She strokes the ribs of the beautiful cage and one of the birds comes to her finger and pecks, pecks, and O it doesn't hurt at all.

APPLES FOR THE
ANIMALS TONIGHT

THE WIND WAS BLOWING mightily when she went out at dusk to feed the pigs. The heat of the house left her quickly. The first star was out there somewhere, would appear. The heat of the house was fueled by their rationed firewood and his plentiful anger, her horrible husband, who had always been horrible, even when, at fifteen, she'd said yes, because there was no other option, because her mother had needed space for the newest child, Harold, another boy, another terror. The ground under her feet had thawed over the past week, but now was growing hard once again, and she stubbed her big toe, inside her thin rubber boot, against a frozen clod of dirt.

Darkness was coming fast. Behind her, the heat of the house awaited her, with her husband made more horrible by age. They were old now together. They'd always been together. He hadn't seemed to see her back hunching day by day but now he saw, now he called her humpbacked in his hard voice, to shame her, to enrage her into changing what she could not.

The pigs in their pen snorted, sensing she was near, coming with her heavy pan of scraps. Peels and cores of apples the fare of the day. She'd put up jars of applesauce and made and froze pies, and still the fruit cellar was piled high with apples, and still the trees in the orchard held ruined fruit frozen and thawed and freezing again. She didn't care about the apples. She didn't care that there were still potatoes in the garden. Or turnips, or beets. She didn't care that spring would arrive some far-off day with its daffodils and its demands. The wind rose again, bringing the winter-iron smell of the freezing pond, where under the surface lived dying creatures, bodies twisting and warping to mark their progress.

THE WOMAN IN THE
WINTER STORM

THROUGHOUT HER BODY, LIES circulated. In her ankles, weak as she crossed the icy road, came the truth: she would make it. The bruising cold boxed her cheeks and the nerve endings in her face protested the lies, singing out that they were in charge. No, she convinced herself: she need not feel the weather's punishment. Her hands curled into the thin pocket linings thudded, too, with her footsteps across the frozen countryside. *Alive, alive.* This is how they found her outside their worm-eaten door: a grotesquely shaped vision in the elements, almost a ghost. And victorious, an old woman who argued amongst her selves and won.

∽FOUR∼

NOW HIS GAMES WERE VERY DIFFERENT
FROM WHAT THEY USED TO BE

PRETTY PAPER SHADES

OVERHEAD SHE LIGHTS, TRYING her best to be bright and bold, a beacon enclosed within the thin shade, pretty pastel paper, appealingly met by the narrow magistrate, he finished with a day's work, come into her room convinced that following her was the obvious choice in the dark, the day's work done, the *where next* otherwise inscrutable unless he were to lie. Overhead, she was. She you. You, she. The next day he had the answer, hindsight read. Where? A house. A house with dark paneling. He was of dark everything, the boy inside always forgotten, insignificant, he who must finish his day's work, following in his father's footsteps, not growing if growing meant looking himself in the eye. He knew the dark shades of shadows, the shoulder of the City, a steep hill that stood indifferent to his efforts. His work the known terrain, a rigorous known, the loss of the work finished, the day's end, the desire for the pretty covered light. The unknown boy inside is really into that, into the pretty paper shades. He wanted her, yes. He wanted the dark-paneled house, yes. He wanted the stretch, the burst, the tear, the flutters of the pretty paper on the wind, the flight of the fragments over the dark shoulder of the City, he inside the house, safe in his father's footsteps, day's work forgotten, the handsome abandoned boy curled into sleep. And she, you.

GENIUSES

THE BOYS ALWAYS PLANNED to be geniuses. Papers spread over the tabletops, numbers on screens. Their gaze has missed something. The girl in a box in the darkness of the closet, hands folded, trinkets worn round her neck, motionless. Once happy to have been on that bus. Who chooses to be anyone's daughter? The plait of her dark hair with an edge to it nearly like a blade. The geniuses can't be forced into looking.

CONFETTI

PAPER DOTS OF VARIOUS hues littered the dark boardroom carpet like confetti. They seemed to be leaking from him, perhaps from some porousness in his scalp. He wouldn't know: he never combed his hair himself. His head felt lighter than ever, nearly airy. He studied the sprinkling over the fibers; they had to be his. In the swaddling silence of the room, there was the sound of nothing. He turned, careful not to shift the orb upon his neck, made his way to the door. From the corner of his eye, he saw a new sprinkling, he was sure, a trail marking his departure. His skull was like the perforated top of a spice jar. Be careful not to knock him over, to spill him all.

CRUCIBLE OF HISTORY

WHEN THEY MET AND began falling in love, she didn't think of it as taking on the weight of another's past. Had she thought of it that way, of the insidious infection of his sorrows, she might at least have paused. Perhaps not. She was in that phase of wanting to be needed.

His history filled him, bulky, as substantial as bones, and seemed able to survive anything, just as bones can survive even the heat of cremation.

When she held her new baby, its pink-skinned helplessness pierced her heart.

She sensed her husband's bewilderment and resentment always shimmering in the room. Forced to choose, she gave her nurturance to the infant.

One might say that this time of putting the baby's needs first was the crucible, when the fire might burn through to reduce the new father's sorrows to ash.

One might hope for a happy ending—certainly when they'd fallen in love that rainy season in the mountains, she'd anticipated, if not happiness, a contentment.

So few truly happy endings, thought their baby when he was grown. He kept his sad history of his missing father to himself, or so he believed.

Walking the trails alone, the dogwoods on the mountainside cluttered with new buds. He was unaware of how his eye, like his father's, looked out for the form of another, a sturdy sunny female, burning bright.

FOR ALL TIME

H E WAS ALWAYS THINKING about what Emma would never do. Maybe that was why, rather than scattering her ashes, he kept them, as if she might experience life vicariously through him.

Before Emma, he was a twenty-six-year-old computer coder who preferred his own company. She was the first woman, the only woman, who'd accepted him for who he was, who filled him with the sense of how home should feel to a kid. Together they hiked the forested hills clustered with wildflowers, red trillium, and ghostly Indian pipes. One day she told him that flowers had male organs, too, and he was astonished that he'd never known that. He must have, though, been exposed to the fact as a student. Why hadn't it ever taken root?

Someday, he promised her, he'd take her to meet his mother, whom he hadn't spoken to since leaving home after high school. Emma didn't understand his avoidance. She, too, had been raised by a single mom. Her gracious perspective was that their mothers had done their best. Emma's generosity of spirit he took as further evidence that her mother, now deceased, had been superior to his. Her mother had raised this wonderful person.

He told Emma he'd overheard his mother, a grocery store cashier, say to a customer, "After you have kids, it all changes. Everything makes sense." He'd been eight years old, sitting on the hard bench beneath the store's plate-glass windows, completing his math homework while waiting for her shift to end as usual.

He'd often wondered what her words might have meant. Her broad smile dimpled her face as she'd spoken, a look she often wore after work hours at home, on her third bottle of beer—a look he'd hated.

Just before Emma passed—naturally she'd die a tragically young death—she said to him that she hoped he would one day have a daughter. That would make him more forgiving of people, she said.

Was that all it was, he countered: a matter of gender?

He drove the four hundred plus miles to see his mother, who knew nothing about the beautiful woman whose ashes were now inurned in the carved olivewood box his mother had once given him apropos of nothing. His mother had been "purging," clearing the attic of the old rickety house by the highway that had belonged to her parents.

Emma, who as a child had lived in dozens of apartments and almost as many cities, had wondered at that, the feeling of growing up in the same one house that both he and his mother had experienced. Emma had wanted to see that pink wooden house.

When his mother opened the door promptly at his knock—clearly she hadn't even looked to see who was on her porch in the twilight—she appeared surprised for only a moment. Her hair was gray, short as a man's, and putty-colored bags hung under her strange violet blue eyes. Her look of disbelief evaporated and her face slackened, before her expression hardened, resolved. With effort, she reached to give him a stiff hug, which he accepted—her body bony and sour-smelling—and stepped back to let him in.

They sat in the living room with its same old, worn furniture, an odor of something like scorched coffee in the air. The red beanbag chair he'd loved to curl up in as a boy hunched in the corner. His mother clicked on a small lamp, and its yellowed shade glowed to reveal a bulb burn. She shifted her slight body on the dumpy beige couch as if willing herself to relax, as if they were simply going to watch a rerun of *The Karate Kid* together again.

He understood then that he'd come to tell her he was sorry. He knew now what it was to be alone.

Her purple-veined hands were clasped in her lap. She raised her head and smiled at him as if in all the silence he'd told her everything.

His hands, crossed over themselves, stretched before him, a gesture of humility he'd never once made before in his long, long life. A life that one day later, turning his back on the pink house for all time, he'd understand had been up to that point quite short. Very short indeed.

OUR LOSSES

WE HAD BEEN ROBBED so many times there was no point in locking up anymore. Anil and I could not afford to replace the TV, so we watched our favorite show on Thursdays down the street at Cosby's. No one at the bar wanted to watch dance, but the owner had taken mercy on us because of all the break-ins—and because I'd agreed to work the late shift on Saturdays. Anything for Anil, who accompanied me on those Saturdays, her sloe eyes growing dreamier and her crooked smile softer as she drank creamy White Russians until closing.

"Aren't you afraid to sleep in that apartment?" asked my mother, when we stopped by to borrow her blender. Anil had started one of her rigorous protein drink regimes, consuming only liquids composed of dark leafy green vegetables and mushy fruits blended with dried whey powder and flaxseed oil. Each concoction was a putrescent-looking shade of puce, but she swore the mixtures kept her brain vibrant and her complexion clear.

Mother would not lend us her blender, fearing it would be stolen. "Come by anytime you like to use it," she told Anil lovingly enough. But going out to the suburbs three times a day? A frown pinched Anil's face.

"Give me another week and I will have you a new blender," I told her on the bus ride home. I'd ask Jerome for extra hours.

Anil shrugged, which might have meant anything. She pulled her paperback out of her bag and began reading. She still had her books. Did thieves ever steal paperbacks? In the dark window, I could see nothing but my own blurry reflection.

I suppose we all believed the thieves would strike again. Yet when we arrived home and looked around the place, I had to admit there was little left to take. An ancient vacuum cleaner, Anil's electric toothbrush, a dented iron no one used. "The thieves have taught us something valuable," I said.

Anil, stretched out across the mattress on the floor, allowed her eyes to finish scanning a line or so before she closed the book on her finger to mark her place. She said, "I hope this is not you making lemonade out of lemons again." Her foot wiggled impatiently, perhaps unconsciously.

I grew warm under her scrutiny. How could I finish?

"Well?" She sighed.

I nodded. "I was going to say that we have learned to live with even less."

I wished I were the sort of man who didn't have to look her in the eyes. A dullness in them became visible to me, and I understood I had been an inattentive student. It would be difficult at first, I thought, as I left for my shift at the bar, but eventually I would have to teach myself to live without her too.

A HOUSE ON THE MARKET

I N THE MONTHS AFTER he left his wife, when he recalled her placid, pale face and unquestioning, almost bovine manner, he experienced what he believed to be a uniquely male mix of pride and regret. The powers a man held over his woman! He lay around his motel room at night, watching ESPN and soft porn, ordering room service, drinking imported beer. Generally, he was satisfied with the separation. Sometimes he went to the bar, passing through an atrium that smelled of bleach. In the bar, blasted with music of thumping bass, he flirted with women who met his standard of attractiveness. His wife had always been good-looking—any man would agree.

Work was going well. Now that he was untethered to the demands of living with another, he could focus completely on his career, which consisted of helping the software company reap greater profits by analyzing mined data. He'd moved up in the corporate ranks. His manager, Sun Lee—who looked like a schoolgirl with her straight, glossy dark hair, pressed white blouses, and slim-fitting skirts—had hinted at another promotion should he continue producing effective cost-saving ideas.

He'd never worried about money, and now, as his savings and investments grew, it appeared he would never need to.

After the first year of his separation passed, he realized a few things. It was time to move out of the motel, find a house. He could hire domestics to provide the conveniences to which he'd become accustomed: laundered crisp linens, rooms tidied and gleaming with sparkling mirrors and glass.

He also realized that he missed his wife in a way he hadn't believed he would. They hadn't spoken, but communicated occasionally—civil, businesslike—through email and the occasional text (such as when he needed her signature on the tax forms his accountant had prepared). Sharp bouts of mourning her absence began to gain in frequency.

When his real estate agent showed him the house on the bluff above Lake Merchant, he stared into the massive hand-built stone fireplace and wished fervently for his wife's opinion. Was this the sort of house he ought to buy? Could he be happy here—that is, reasonably so? Who was ever *thoroughly* happy? Though hadn't she been, his tranquil wife—hadn't that been the source of her serenity, her level gaze on his face?

In the cool living room, he took his phone from his pocket and began to text her, a strange thudding in his stomach as if his heart had dropped from its cage to stir everything in his body from this lower depth. The real estate agent, a beefy man with the look of a quarterback early retired by a blown knee, discreetly stepped out to have another look at the details of the gourmet kitchen, as he put it.

The text grew in length. He was rambling, repeating himself, thanking her in various ways for her unflinching trust in him, faith he hadn't deserved and had in fact betrayed. He read and reread his words, adding and deleting, working to craft the best, *only* message of his life to his wife, over whom, it was obvious to him now, he'd possessed not one iota of power.

The man in the kitchen cleared his throat. It was getting late, yes.

Yes, that's right, he had a meeting with Sun Lee within the half hour. An image of his boss arose in his mind: Sun Lee tapping a well-manicured pink fingernail on the conference table before her, a bemused smile spreading over her face at the thought of what he was about to do—had almost done. He returned the phone to his pocket.

I'M AN EXPERT ON

- when he's evading the issue
- when he thinks he's being funny but his humor is obscuring the issue
- when he's withholding information
- when he's had a pleasing interaction with Suki at the office
- when he didn't get to meet Suki for lunch
- when he's spotted Suki in the café with Bruce
- when he's eaten something that doesn't agree with him for lunch
- when traffic on the commute home was brutal and he had more time than ever in his head and his head was filled with images of Suki smiling at Bruce while deftly picking up sushi rolls with chopsticks poised in her delicate fingers, pretty pink nails gleaming under the café's hanging lights
- when he despairs that we are aging, us, a couple well-matched to the extent that the matching feels too much like sameness, and comfort and contentment just aren't enough
- when the world seems apocalyptic and who knows how many days are left and he may wind up in a ditch by the side

of the road, no water, no rain, dead blistered skin shredding, the shreds surrounding his festering body food for creatures he's too weak to repel, and the last images burned into the back of his mind's eye—the only part of him actually seeing, retinas long lost to the scorching elements—are visions of Suki, dear Suki, beautiful beautiful breathing Suki

PROMISE

MAGNETIC BREATH: YOURS WITH these new mints, and you'll draw every male from miles around into your private hemisphere. They'll waste no time padding to you softly like tomcats, noses to the wind, twitchy-whiskered, circling around you, tails held high, no idea what you've got but you've definitely got something, this they know. You'll smile that beatific smile, enigmatic and bright, the star of your own favorite movie. For once you won't need to concentrate on perfect posture, holding your shoulders high and tummy in. Your luxurious hair will cascade down your shapely back in soft voluminous waves, radiant highlights glinting celestially. You won't even need to speak, but say that you deigned to—what pearls will trip from your tongue in melodious silver tones! Soon the room will crowd with adoring fans, thrilled to be within range, hovering, anxious to be of service. If you will only put out your hand, softest of supple roseate flesh, you will find it filled with your heart's desires, even those you couldn't have stooped to imagine.

❧FIVE❧

IF SHE DIDN'T LIKE IT, WHY,
THE WORLD WAS WIDE, AND THERE
WERE MANY OTHER PLACES SHE COULD GO

CONFECTION

S HE DISCOVERED A RECIPE for lemon sherbet written on a stained index card in the cupboard of her uncle's kitchen. She didn't know whose handwriting made up the crabbed lines. She didn't know her uncle, never had, the childless uncle who'd died and left the property to her. He'd left the gardener to her as well, or at any rate, Ramon didn't want to leave. He appeared to sleep in the little shack she thought better suited to sheltering the tools.

When she found the recipe, she asked Ramon to gather the Meyer lemons that had dropped onto the back patio before he climbed up the hill to clip back wild vegetation she had yet to see or identify. She didn't know the property's flora or fauna—she imagined wildlife roamed the overgrown acres.

She planned to start caring about all that in January. Also on the agenda for next year: consider Daniel's request that she return to the city and give their relationship another try.

Perhaps she would reconsider all her relationships. Through the kitchen window, she saw the light appear in Ramon's shed. In the distance, the light was tiny, like a faraway star.

The sound of her guests, old friends from the city, swelled on the patio. She couldn't remember when she'd acquired the friendships.

The lemon sherbet she'd made was melting all over the counter, puddling into grooves between the dark tiles. She was sorry she'd forgotten the confection, now unservable.

Laughter drifted from the patio where her guests crunched pistachios, guzzled champagne, caressed one another's thighs under the white-clothed table. Sherbet was unimportant. She could go up to bed now if she chose. Someone would surely blow out the candles.

Pascal had sewn a parchment note into his jacket pocket to aid him in remembering his visions of God. He'd understood his revelations would fade.

CUTTING GARDEN

THE INHERENT DANGERS OF growing wildflowers: bee stings, if you're allergic; hyper-awareness about rainfall leading possibly to addiction to the TV weather channel (all those smiley-face sun symbols), which means purchasing a TV in the first place; becoming an expert on irrigation systems, which means finding a mentor who turns out to be Raul, a dark-haired man who lives the next town over in a neat adobe house with blue trim, with his shapely wife, who, like her house, displays bright blue accents (eyes, ribbon-strapped sundress), which you learn when you pass by one day, driven perhaps by your guilt after a month of afternoons with Raul that have nothing to do with the watering of flowers but involve another garden of pleasures that often seem heavenly in nature. Not earth-bound.

Your flowers thrive, so well that you are furnishing every farmer's market in a hundred-mile radius with Cut Flowers by Clara, making more money than you thought possible and coming face to face with the fact that you are not, after all, a ne'er-do-well, something your father pronounced the final time you quit college. Suddenly, you must learn about profit margins and investments, not to mention bookkeeping, and so enter Blake, a financial wizard who lives in a sophisticated high-rise in the city with, it turns out, his classy fiancée, who wears knee-high boots of polished leather and a belted beige coat tailored to show off her trim figure when she steps from under the apartment's awning into the awaiting taxi. You never meant to discover her, to espy the apartment itself, but something vaguely disturbing from those sunny afternoons with Raul lingered when, after the monthly statements were reconciled, Blake advised you, albeit not with words, to take pleasure trips with him now and again.

It happens. A deep sting.

After a lengthy wait in the reception area with a loud TV, where no one cares about the weather forecast, the doctor sees you, his smiling face another kind of sun as he assures you you're not allergic. One thing leads to another and he recommends a book on learned optimism, his sure hand offering you his card on which he's scribbled the title, and he doesn't wear a ring but you know if you drive by his five-bedroom Tudor in the elm-shaded neighborhood, the lights that glow through the dining room window will reveal an elegant figure seated at the other end of the table, lifting her glass to his.

His card. You break it down, you chew and chew, the blue ink of the title sluicing in the pulp, while you cross the office parking lot to where your pickup with its bed full of cut flowers awaits the next market.

BABY BIRD

GRAY SHEETS, GRIME, CHILL of metal. Smell of ancient burned toast. What's a home anyway? Outside, a nest fallen from the tree whose roots heave the sidewalk. Why doesn't the nest fall to pieces? Caught inside the bowl of twigs and purloined strangers' hair, the darkish down of the absent bird. The girl is eight, maybe ten. Bare head, bare arms, bare legs. It's February. Bare feet, one cut and bleeding. Bloody footprints shaped like valentine hearts track over the porch steps, from door to tree. Tree to door. Door like a waiting maw. Inside, scattered glass, shards large and small. Deathly quiet now. Smell of ancient burnt toast. The soiled sheets. Where is the bird? Where did she go?

MAGICIAN'S ASSISTANT

Her mother looked at her as if with eyes that could pin her to the wall. She hadn't cleaned up all the scraps from cutting out her paper dolls, her mother made her see that now. She stooped to pick up the white fragments from the red tiles beside the kitchen table. Her mother's voice hissed above. It was time to set the table for dinner. She was too young to know what powers men held over women, how raw loneliness could simmer inside a woman, though she could sense something underneath her mother's hatred.

Her mother rapped the scissors against the top of her skull, the heavy blades stinging her crown. She took the bits of paper to the trash can. Her mother closed the scissors away high in the cabinet and told her it would be some time before she would be allowed to use them again.

She set the table for three, plates, silverware, and napkins, carefully, quietly, quickly. She was talented. She could be the lady in the box in the magic show, all glitter, and smiling while the magician closed the lid on her and sawed through the wood, the audience fearful and then gasping when the man reopened the box to show that she had disappeared.

DAYLILIES

A N HOUR REMAINED BEFORE her scheduled phone call with her mother. She sat in the armchair in the corner of the living room, turned to the crossword in the Sunday *Times*, and absorbed herself in the puzzle. All the answers to the clues seemed to align with questions she expected to hear in the upcoming conversation. And then the phone rang, and within moments her mother asked if she'd met her new husband at a bar, and she had to answer yes. She didn't want to admit it, but it seemed important not to lie.

What had been the rush to get married, her mother wanted to know, as she too had wondered. But her husband had said, *Let's throw caution to the wind*, his dark eyes sparkling so appealingly that she was convinced in that moment it was time she stopped being so careful, always trying to live by reason. Her heart was growing and growing, she felt, ready to leap out of her. They lay in his bed, the covers a complicated landscape of furrows and ridges blurring next to her eye. He caressed the wing of her shoulder blade, the shadows in the room purpling, and she agreed: they'd go to City Hall the next morning. Yes, he'd move into her apartment; obviously they couldn't live together in this room he rented in a stranger's house, with its water-stained dark paneling and single cloudy overhead light bulb.

The following day, the magistrate performed the rites with a vacant expression on his handsome face, stumbling over the words, and when he finished, gave her a particularly knowing and appreciative look. *What was that?* her new husband demanded once they were outside the building. They'd paused to photograph themselves before the thick stand of tall daylilies that grew in a circular bed in the center of the pale brickwork. They'd want the image. They'd want to say to one another, remember? Remember that day, ninety degrees, women sweating, men's faces pasty, the orange of the flowers shrill in the overcast sky? But that's not what they'd think about.

The picture would show him wearing a narrow quizzical smile.

Hers would be more inscrutable unless you really knew her. If you did, you'd see it was the smile of a girl who was trying to convince herself that a boy was everything she wanted him to be.

But who can live in the territory of hindsight with its perfect, monotonous terrain?

As she talked to her mother she could picture the vibrant lilies and knew her mother would appreciate the sight, but her tongue lay dead in her mouth. Her mother had always admonished her to plan ahead, think what might happen. Her mother would never see the photo. Never.

LIME TREE

SHE BUYS A NEW house with a lime tree, and she has much to learn. A book advises minimal pruning of citrus trees. But that is not to say that the trimming of branches needn't be done. So she prunes her lime tree, carefully removing branches that crowd the light and impede the possibility of blossoms. Already so many limes on the ground!

If her mother lived here instead of across the country, they would drink margaritas on the patio, a bright green slice of the fruit attached to their glasses' rims, bake key lime pies with browned meringue. Together they'd take paper bags of the fruit to the neighbors. Her gregarious mother would enjoy this, a Saturday morning stroll through the neighborhood, ringing the doorbells. She doesn't even know if her mother likes limes. She's sent her mother pictures of the tree bearing fruit, but her mother has never said.

When she visited her mother last, she stood in the shadows at the door of the den and watched her mother sleep, the dream gently waving through her body, fluttering her fingers near her face. In the close room, a tart odor pervaded like an opaque mist, as if she were standing in her own backyard next to the lime tree, enveloped in the morning fog.

Please put off dying until I no longer disappoint you, she thought. Her mother's blue eyes opened, and her mother looked at her the way little girls do when you tell them the truth.

ABANDONING THE BIRDS

To look at her mother when her mother was unable to see her was strange. She might have wished for this when she was a girl. Her mother, in the middle of the bed, had always been small but now she was round, puffed and white like the bloated underbelly of a beached fish. The huge bed filled what had been the dining room in the country house. Her mother lay on her back, head turned toward the window that was filled with gloom, eyes closed, mouth hanging open. She studied her mother's face as if she'd never seen it before, and perhaps in a way she hadn't.

When she was growing up in the apartment in the city where they'd lived together, her eyes had often fixated on a pink birthmark on her mother's cheek, a splotch that flushed red when her mother was angry. But inspecting her mother's face under the glow of the bedside lamp now, she saw that mark had faded into nothingness. Soft innocent eyelids, veined, covered her mother's eyes, eyes the blue of cut topaz with a dangerous glitter. When she'd been a girl, she'd dreaded those eyes turning on her.

Somewhere in the forested distance, a dog barked, and closer to the house, birds called. Jays nested close in craggy branches that reached ceaselessly for the roof. When her mother had moved here last year, she'd filled the substantial yard with bird feeder after bird feeder, fifteen or more, and bought seed in bulk that she had to transport to each site in a wheelbarrow. Now the feeders were empty, the birds left to fend for themselves. You weren't supposed to begin feeding birds if you weren't going to keep it up.

PAINTING FOR MY MOTHER

I PAINTED A PICTURE of a meal for my mother. Green peas on a white plate with blue shadows. A wine glass, full of red, its stem long and thin. I had never painted a still life before. I don't know what I thought I was doing. She had always enjoyed eating and could no longer. Maybe I wanted to sweeten the drip of the morphine. Maybe I wanted her to remember what she no longer desired. Perhaps it was merely something that I could do. When I took the painting to her bed, in what had once been the dining room, a ghost of a smile traversed her ashen face. Her eyes still burned bright, the blue of the parakeet that had been my pet when I was a child. Then, she was always cleaning up scattered birdseed and tiny feathers, and she'd never had it in her to tell me that I wasn't going to train the bird to speak. That was one dream she'd allowed me. Or perhaps she shared in the dream despite herself.

She closed her eyes and snored lightly. I positioned the painting on the easel where she could see it when she opened her eyes. I believed she would do that.

IN THE BEGINNING

I.
Breath came to me as it comes to us all, unsolicited but grasped at. Something in us, animals, wants it, evidently.

II.
In the beginning there was a man and a woman. In the beginning there is always a man and a woman. Some say one day a woman will be able to conceive a child without a man, men will be entirely unnecessary. Some say this is fantasy, a pipe dream. Consider the pipe dream. A pipe requires inhalation. Let the man puff his pipe, contemplating parthenogenesis, reproduction without fertilization, virgin birth. The man is okay with Jesus, but he doesn't really believe in Mary. Parthenogenesis occurs naturally in certain plant and insect species (aphids, bees, and ants), and like many other procedures, can now occur with the assistance of scientists. Captive domestic chickens, pythons, sharks, komodo dragons, lizards, and certain birds can reproduce parthenogenetically. Women will produce females only. Put that in your pipe and smoke it, some women might say.

III.
Her father likes to tell the story of her beginning, as a blue baby. She has heard it two times before, a memorable magnitude when it comes

to her taciturn father. In the latest telling she discovers that when he heard the doctor say *it was a girl* while handing over the blue body with the umbilical cord wrapped round and round her neck, her father thought she died. But then she began to squawk. *Squawk,* her father repeats, relishing that word. A kind of debasement of the whole human enterprise. Her mother gives a sidelong smile and says he doesn't like to show his feelings. But that's not quite right. He doesn't like to show certain kinds of feelings. He isn't one for sentiment. He isn't convinced he's necessary, but he would like her to believe so. He has given up smoking and his breath is even and slow.

HANDHOLDING

IN THE HOSPITAL, HER mother lies in the bed hooked up to oxygen, to monitors, to various equipment, blinking and hissing. Her father asks the pastor for a prayer and they three take hands as if by instinct. The ridges in her father's large thick hands have softened with age, but barely. The time she was five and reached to take his hand as they walked down their gravel driveway, somehow not noticing the lit cigarette he held. The skin next to the knuckle of her forefinger burned, leaving a raised disk-shaped scar that she carries still, forty years later. He was so upset that he would not hold her hand again. Until now.

In her other hand, the flesh and bones of the pastor, a whip-thin man who avoids her eyes, bows his head, and imparts specific words that surprise her. A petition that the inert figure of her mother be healed, that her mother return home to serve the congregation. She expected words of ambiguity, an acknowledgment of God's omnipotence, that He knew what was best, life on earth or wherever.

Her father clings to her hand and she can almost physically feel his wishing, in the fevered way that children long for what they believe is within their grasp. Where once there'd been only deadened skin, the scar on her hand takes on sensation. His hand in hers now, all these years later, an unconscious wish fulfilled. The sound of a TV plays in another room.

IS THERE NO ONE WHO LISTENS?
(IF ONLY THE WEATHER GOT BETTER)

Another hour of PT with Joe. Tricks to show me how to get fine-tuning with my hand.

My diet was changed to mechanical soft, liquids with a straw.

The caseworker was in.

I can get out of bed myself.

Everything's setting in. It's going to be harder than I thought.

I had to wring out the washcloth for my face. They tied up my good hand.

It feels pretty good, sitting up, feels like I have some power.

Tell your husband I'm not going to get discouraged.

Things are looking up. I can use my mouth more.

All these little tricks can do a lot for you.

I'm not going to regress by getting down in the dumps.

I walked sixty-five feet down the hall.

Another swallowing test soon. I choked today.

I'm coming along.

I got your gift. It's something pretty to look at and enjoy.

How can I put this best? I'm excited to go home but unsure of myself.

All day I'm feeling nostalgic.

If I start to cry I might never stop.

I feel like I accomplished something, walking up those steps.

Your dad thinks we can handle it together.

So eager to go home and be warm when I want to be.

I walked with my cane. I rode the bike for five miles.

Everything looked so beautiful when I came home, even uptown when we drove through it, all gray and dismal.

I'm having my ups and downs with my disposition. I have to overcome that. It worries your dad.

I'm lucky I don't have to relearn everything.

It's a dismal dreary drab day. Ice on the trees.

I can't do anything to anyone's satisfaction.

We went to Ideal Market and I walked down the aisles and I couldn't believe how big it was.

I haven't had any tears today.

I'm running out of things to say.

Does what I'm saying make sense? I know it sounds strange.

It's amazing how feelings change from one day to the next.

That was a day I don't want to repeat.

I did my papers this morning. The whole point is to make you think.

My thinking process is pretty good. I don't have any way of knowing if my answers are right without my nurse telling me.

I'd like to wear my own underwear.

Sun is shining real bright today in the windows.

More paperwork. It's something to think about, make your brain work.

I'd like to know what I can do.

Each time you read a paragraph you learn something.

Your dad and I ended up getting angry with each other. It's better that I let him do it.

The snow came down today.

Whatever they suggest, Dad said, we'll follow.

I thought, Holy Toledo!

When they visited me in isolation they said I was funny. I hope I wasn't rude.

I don't have the strength to run the curling brush on my hair.

My hair looks like the rest of me now, down the tubes.

If the weather just got nice, we could jump in the car and take off and go somewhere.

It's important to know what's happening outside the door, so I scan the newspaper.

I'll try listening to books tomorrow.

I like the books you gave me; they're different.

I'm finding the word search books more and more interesting.

I was having a little problem drawing a line around the words, had to use a straight edge.

I have some kind of angel looking out for me.

Anyway, the game looks like fun.

Life is not sweet right now.

It's coming easier.

The card you sent me is on the desk. I look at it all the time.

I don't remember you brushing my hair.

Is there no one who listens?

SOURCE OF THE ACCIDENT

H ER PARENTS WERE WAITING it out in the apses of their minds where everything remained the same and death would come only as an incremental change, or so seemed their hope. They actively prepared for a heavenly afterlife, getting involved in a church: weekly services, deacon and deaconess, Bible study, choir, socials. Her father maintained the sign on the church front, posting religious bon mots. Her parents worked hard on their forgiveness.

But God forgave or made trouble as the mood struck.

One day her mother suffered several strokes, and her father was in hysterics, the boy in him who'd never been loved in charge now. The color of his eyes shifted from coal to hazel.

The pastor entered the hospital room where her mother slept under a pink cashmere blanket someone had brought, and her father asked the man to say a prayer. The three of them encircled the sleeping figure of her mother, joining hands, and the pastor intoned words while her father wept. It was December, cold; outside, snow fell from the gray Midwestern sky. Back home the temperature was in the sixties, sun shining over the Monterey pines, madrones, and manzanitas.

One morning, after the danger had passed and just before she was to return home, her mother turned to her father, her hair standing out from her skull, crispy as if seared by the misfirings in her brain, and said that this, her strokes, had all been her own fault. As if he knew already what her mother would say before she'd finished her sentence, her father, eyes locked into her mother's, began shaking his head.

Her mother's blue eyes, once glacial, were liquid, a color like what must have been the hue of the oceans at the birth of the world, nearly pure, as in the pure idea of pure beauty. Her mother's face relaxed and her eyes closed.

This attunement of her parents: a private act. She looked away, at the closed drapes, a tremor pulsing through her.

When she returned home, the year was coming to an end. She gazed out the window where an odd light of a bluish cast glowed across the lawn. The strange light seemed to have no source, but of course was only some phenomenon with a scientific explanation, perhaps simply the gleam of the moon refracted through the redwoods.

She looked out, haunted by the innocence of her parents in their lamb-like softness, those once fierce and frightening people who'd had to raise her. She'd glimpsed the spark of the source of the accident of her existence, impossible now to unsee.

HOUSE IN THE DESERT

THE DESERT'S VIBRANT BLOOMING cacti had attracted her first. In the shimmering white air, even the towering rocks seemed to breathe. She makes her home in the desert now, takes pride in the closest town's designation as an International Dark-Sky Community. But every several months she makes the sojourn to the house of her childhood in the Northeast, to the tiny village surrounded by forest and crisscrossed with streams. Her father lives in the same wood-sided house where she grew up, white with painted blue shutters swollen and warped from rain, snow, and heat.

When she enters the house, her father—once a man sturdy as the trees he felled—holds her and cries. She loves and hates this, that it took him nearly fifty years to learn to hug her. Half a century. Another few decades for her to acclimate to the change is out of the question, and she wishes she could simply accept the awkward demonstration, forget the long past.

She carries her bag to her room: pale yellow walls, a muted print cover on the narrow bed. An arrangement of silk flowers in a white wicker basket in the corner, added once the room became used for guests. On the dresser top sits someone's perfume, a gold bracelet. A china dish holds a tortoiseshell barrette, two pennies, a faded receipt. Fluffy bright rugs cover the floorboards, texture under her bare feet.

She has always loved to go shoeless. You can't, really, in the desert. She leaves her bag unopened and returns to the kitchen.

Her father and she sit at the old oak table and sip cups of black tea. She tells him about the research she's read on drinking tea. All good news: the habit promotes health. They say nothing about the company who owns the rights to the earth beneath their feet, about the dying town, villagers pale and sorry. She's doing that thing again, wanting to make him happy.

Then he opens his mouth in a terrible smile that squeezes her heart. Struggling not to sob this time, as each time, he begins the story. He was there that morning in the hospital. In those times the father wasn't wanted, but the doctor appeared in the waiting room and pointed at him: *I need you.* When finally the doctor had her out, the gray gristled cord wrapped round her neck, how blue she was. Not a sound from her for the longest time. He breaks down.

Through his fingers he says something that sounds like *tell me my great day gave you a reason.*

She murmurs soothing affirmations. Eventually her breath calms, pulse rate restored.

She's aging too. She has her own stories. She has a house in the desert. Shelter from the extremes. In the mornings, the stone floors are frigid. Slippers essential.

Under the table, she presses her bare feet together, one warm foot to the other. No need to think about what's going on underground. Imperative not to. She rests her hand on her father's forearm, holds herself here.

GREEN GLASS BIRD

THERE ARE MOMENTS WHEN she can't speak in the world. Not even to friends. The friend she'd had for a few years, her husband, her best friend once. What about that tragic marriage? Her father remembers and sleeps down the hall behind an old door that sticks in the frame, the sound of him a presence large and soft. In this room under the haunted look of the angel atop the fir tree, lights winking, the tree is dying, and the world is, along with her, awaiting a new chance, a new year, a new number.

Years ago, her daughter had a bed and, like any child, no past and no future. They'd hung on the tree a green glass bird, said to sleep, thought to dream when wrapped in tissue in the attic until the next year. Her father remembers and sleeps large and soft down the hall.

A strand of tinsel fallen on the carpet.

Her daughter is a woman with a past now, her own father, and the green glass bird she might hang on a fir tree.

She never meant to wind up in her father's house, her daughter lost, herself an intruder in her own dreams, holding fragments of her past like the glittering shards of a glass ornament in her palm. Barely discernible beside a red-laced cut, the shape of a small sharp wing.

～SIX～

HE TRIED TO SAY HIS PRAYERS BUT
ALL HE COULD REMEMBER WERE
HIS MULTIPLICATION TABLES

ONE EARLY
SUMMER MORNING

My FATHER GLANCED OVER at her still form on the bed, a mound of layered covers of varying weights, textures, and shades. *I'm under here somewhere*, perhaps my mother was thinking. "She's going to wake," he said. He rubbed his elbows. "But then, you never know." His voice teased playfully. He wanted to seem offhand, casually indifferent. But over the past months since my mother's stroke, he'd known every move that lady made, his wife of over fifty years. Knew if she'd forgotten her vitamins in the morning, knew when she ought to sit down and read the paper for a while, when it was time for her manicure.

He must have sensed she would not move again that summer morning. He had to have known. Always protecting himself with his little jokey remarks. She appeared frozen. Already, not even 8 a.m., the temperature had risen so high that the back of my neck was damp with perspiration, and the thin beige blouse I wore wanted to cling to my moist body. A smell of sour milk, of decaying stems of chrysanthemums. Overpowering. Inescapable. In a corner on the table near the window sat a forgotten vase of grocery-store flowers with a scant layer of cloudy water cooking in the sun. So that was what she'd last been given.

My two brothers, with their identical mustaches and ponytails and smoldering eyes, stood to either side of the bed and avoided looking into one another's faces. Her favorites, sons, the eldest and the baby, lifelong rivals. One of them had brought the cheap bouquet and the other was furious that he hadn't. As the outsider, I preferred my role as just a girl, only a girl, insignificant, easily disregarded and discounted. My brothers stared at my father like children who want to believe in the authority of a parent despite the evidence of their own eyes.

So it was that our mother died, some early hour, July, amidst our rage and without our consent.

UNRAVELED

HER SWEATER LAY ACROSS the bed. To look at the shape of it and see her in it, how the weave had taken on the form of her body, that tender stretch of the sleeves—the way she always pushed them up her forearms. The sweater was a sweet red, the hue of poppies, of a particular strata of the clouds at sunset. The sweater on the bed. As if she'd been here only this morning, last evening at the latest. He walked around the room carefully on the balls of his naked feet, silent, but creatures in the walls felt his tentativeness. His restraint.

She'd always sung in the room. She just did that, sang as she went around the whole place, unselfconscious. He'd never known anyone like her, who didn't give it a second thought, and he wondered now at why everyone in the world was so silent. The room was so silent now.

Her sweater lay across the bed. He passed it again and again, and he would keep passing it, unless he dove into it and filled his nostrils with her smell, a scent of musk and something he couldn't name, perhaps a spice, a plant, a perfume he didn't know. He knew so little. He was coming to understand that.

He would never be able to move the sweater from the bed. Though he knew he would have to one day. By then it would unravel, and when it did, what would he do? He who was already undone, the weave of himself a loose scrabble of threads.

HOBBYIST REPAIRMAN

SOMETHING MAKES HIM TICK. He functions on his own mechanisms of polyphonic calibers, weights and gauges of doubt. Scattered across his workbench: scraps of clocks, gutted but saved. A rusted, bent second hand, shattered glass face, tarnished cogs, dirty wheels. To what end? What will happen when all the clocks are gone?

REPOSITORY

HE KEEPS A DARK-FRAMED photograph in the chest in his living room, a picture that for many years held a place on the papered wall of his mother's bedroom. The flocked wallpaper is long gone, as is the room, as is his mother. He has this portrait. Black and white, soft-focused. He knows nothing about photography, the art and science of how a photographer knows to capture light. Sometimes when he can bear the fossilized guilt he takes the picture out of its mahogany tomb. In the citrusy sunlight he looks into the face of the young woman, his mother, naked but for the dreams in her eyes. The baby, him, attached to her breast as if he will never let go.

ECHO

Juan's boyfriend Douglas was an orderly at the new hospital, like him, and they both were infected with the optimism that the new equipment, clean walls, and shining floors engendered. Sometimes they ate in the cafeteria, excited over the shared secret of their relationship, though Juan worried others would notice that their trays held duplicate orders of Cobb salad and iced tea, and guess they were more than friends.

Douglas possessed a full head of brush-cut gray hair, dark fathomless eyes, razor stubble that overtook his cheeks each day by three in the afternoon. Often, elderly people on the ward mistook him, with his grave air and somber expression, for a doctor. Juan thought Douglas handsome in a way that defied categorization, and believed that his boyfriend's good looks infused his own appearance. When he looked into the mirror at his gleaming dark hair and striking blue eyes, he saw a younger-looking, more urbane man—he hadn't realized how fine he truly was, until Douglas.

The newness of the hospital faded and the facility became no more than the worksite they dragged themselves to, groggy-eyed, before the sun, merely another brick façade looming up from St. Charles Street. So, too, dulled their once incandescent relationship. Juan reminisced about their first date, the swanky restaurant, thick white tablecloths, candlelight. At Douglas's insistence, he'd ordered the pheasant. How could Douglas have known he would savor the gamy, oily flesh, something he'd never tasted, never cared to?

Their beginning was forever ago, history, as were Douglas's three wives whose names Juan didn't remember, perhaps had never even heard. Now he wondered if Douglas had loved them fiercely too, just before walking out on them.

I don't want to drift away from us, he said, in a last effort. Douglas paused to listen. It was evening; they'd both had to work late, neither had eaten dinner. They stood in the dim kitchen, shadows from the overhead lights obscuring the doors of the expensive cabinets. Once he'd loved these cabinets with a foolish, inane fervor. Now he envisioned how barren they would be, devoid of Douglas's dishes, pots, and pans, his crock pot and the fondue maker they'd used twice.

Douglas only smiled vacantly, stepped forward to squeeze his shoulder, and gave him a dry kiss on the top of his head. He closed the door after him carefully, the soft click of the lock loud in the kitchen.

Juan stood looking at the handsome image of himself reflected in the shiny range hood, all he had left.

YOU CAN DO ANYTHING

CECILIA LEFT ME ONE sunny Saturday afternoon in September, a perfect autumn day. I didn't know how to be intimate, my wife said. She longed for the fulfillment of a soul mate. Though she'd once believed I was her kindred spirit, our past six years of marriage had proved otherwise. Three weeks later I saw her walking out of Greenway's Books downtown with a man who couldn't have been more than twenty-five to her thirty-four, the two wrapped around each other as if huddled for warmth. It was seventy-eight degrees. Cecilia was laughing—I saw that right off—blushing, bra-less.

The guy sported a spunky grin above his scraggly beard, which he no doubt wore to make himself appear older, and seemed haplessly merry. I believe they were telling jokes. His gaze was locked into hers: co-dependent.

The pockets on Cecilia's thin lavender blouse shimmied as she walked, and a breeze lifted her brilliant red hair from her shoulders. She wore several necklaces, mostly silvery chains, though I noted a few colored gemstones. A long flowing skirt hid her lithesome legs, but I knew they were under the silky fabric. In that moment, I was self-consciously aware of everything that had to do with the corporeal and nothing at all with her soul.

As we neared one another, I desperately discarded comments I might make to indicate concern for her well-being. Her progress in her spiritual quest.

"Henry, what a surprise!" Cecilia did look astonished. Chagrined, too, I later decided. "This is Doug," she said.

The guy unwillingly but complaisantly turned his attention away from my beautiful wife—ah, ex-wife-to-be—to acknowledge my presence. Curiosity intermingled with annoyance in his expression. Clearly, Cecilia had spoken of me.

I presented my hand for a courteous handshake. "Good afternoon, Doug." I examined his mien, his bearing, his style in togs. He wore a long-sleeved chambray button-down too warm for the weather, dark pants also too warm, and, perhaps in an attempt at keeping cool, ill-advisedly, Birkenstocks that displayed his troll-like feet and hairy toes. His hair needed cutting and his abundant nostril hair trimming. This could not be Cecilia's idea of her soul mate.

To return the handshake, he shuffled the items he carried, slinging a canvas bag by its strap over his shoulder and switching a small white bag that held some sort of baked treat to his left hand. He leaned forward extending his hand, and the bag slid from his shoulder, spilling books onto the sidewalk.

"Oops!" Cecilia emitted a high-pitched trill. She giggled nervously as she bent to the pavement, and the quality of her laughter took on a breathy sound as she gathered books. She suffered from asthma and I hoped she wasn't going into an attack. Was she carrying her inhaler? I couldn't ask: the question had always infuriated her, as had any mention of her condition.

I helped them—*her*—retrieve *Your Personal Stones* and *Finding Future Crystal Paths* and who knew what other ridiculous tomes. "What is all this?" I asked. I'd been aware of her fascination with crystals, but I had little patience with such gimmicks.

Cecilia held a compact disc, *Sounds of Nature: The Ocean.* The clear plastic cover was cracked. Flushing, she tossed her head. A bit defiantly, I would have said later. Her dangling earrings bounced and flashed, and I realized what the pale colored stones were.

"Ah!" I reached for a crystal earring. "You're wearing your future?"

Later, when I mulled back over the incident, I thought perhaps I shouldn't have made the last remark. However, in self-defense, the comment slipped out in the moment of a surprising discovery. And hadn't Cecilia always complained that one of my faults was an inability to be spontaneous?

"*This* is none of your business, Henry." She pulled her head away to distance the earring from my fingers. The light pink stone—rose quartz, I learned—appeared to contain jagged edges, and I hoped she didn't sleep with them in her ears. She often wore jewelry to bed, losing items amongst the covers.

Doug looked disapprovingly at me. "You're not supposed to let anyone touch your crystal." He seemed sincerely distressed. Cecilia made a consoling sound in her throat and petted his arm. Before me. In plain sight.

"I don't want to know what will happen. Spare me the details." I turned away.

I took a step or two, then pivoted to face them. Encouraged by my new-found lucidity in the moment, I may have gotten carried away. "As far as I'm concerned, the worst has already happened."

I retreated back down First Street, no longer in the mood for lunch at Pete's, solitary in the booth that I'd been inhabiting far too regularly, my stomach a shrunken, cold stone now. I could have sworn I heard Cecilia say, "Poor Henry."

November arrived, bringing rain. Wet leaves, burgundy and gold, adhered to the steep-pitched sidewalks of our Shadyside neighborhood, the slickness a peril if one weren't paying attention and stepped too quickly, I knew from experience. The year before, I'd taken a nasty tumble jogging. Twilight, I'd been hurrying to beat nightfall when I slid on a layer of slimy leaves and fractured my ankle. Only a slight chip fracture, the orthopedist found, but I'd had to wear a cast for six weeks and, after its removal, forewent exercise for another two.

"You should try yoga," Cecilia had suggested, as I grew more irritable without the runner's high I depended on to counteract the stress of my job. No one visits a financial counselor until they are in deep trouble, and by then, the news I have to impart is not good. People still think there's some magical solution, however. They don't want to hear that they're going to have to change their spending habits any more than I want to tell them that change is the only solution.

Cecilia in her yoga gear was a vision. In her leotards, her curvaceous body moved so gracefully, so fluidly, charging the very atoms of the air in our cozy house. She did not appreciate my compliments, however. I was simply incapable of moving beyond the physical, she felt. She withdrew, sexually.

I became meaner. "Tell me, exactly when do endorphins kick in for the yogi? After the fourth or fifth *ohm*, perhaps?" I knew full well she did not make such sounds when she practiced her postures. *Asanas*, that is, as she'd corrected me many times. If I'd have once used the proper word, would that have changed her feelings? Softened her heart toward me?

A reflexive dirty look had already become hers by then. She was well aware of the habit—it vexed her to no end and she wanted to overcome it. I watched her struggle to contain her expression, wanting to shout, "Come on, Cecilia, be spontaneous! Don't hold back! Let me see your disgust! Let it out, let it all out!" Yet, my heart wasn't in the fight. I knew what I wanted from her was passion of another kind, and I knew I wasn't going to get it.

Eventually she grew practiced at transforming her looks of aversion into a kind of determined apathy. But the daily washed-out looks of sadness, her melancholia, are what I remember most about the last of our days together. "We're just not meant to be, Henry." According to her, there was no blame. It was a fate of the Cosmos. She cried when she said that if I wouldn't take my part in our separating, she would have no choice but to leave on her own.

When, oh when, had she changed? Where was my first little slip, miscalculation? Try as I might, I could not discover when the shift began. I think of my first alarm clock, a Big Ben windup: I'd had to observe it running for a time first to determine if it ran fast or slow, there being no way to know until the gap presented itself. One can adjust a clock. Cecilia would not allow me to do *any* correcting. Our lack of synchronicity just *was.* "Accept it, Henry, please."

She never knew that I'd attended two Hatha Yoga classes. I went on my lunch hour, a Tuesday and Thursday. I'd paid the full fee for six weeks of classes, intending to go. Besides the fact that it was more economical to pay for the entire series at once, I'd figured if I paid all the money up front, I would feel obligated if for no other reason than financial pragmatism. However, some commitments one can't manipulate oneself into keeping.

I fell asleep in Thursday's class at the end during the meditation. A fat woman in a jade green leotard, sitting on the mat beside mine, scared the hell out of me when she placed her hand on my shoulder. "You're snoring," she whispered into my face when I jerked straight up, eyes shocked open. Her breath smelled of garlic. She smiled and had tiny teeth with gaps between them.

The sensation of jerking awake in a public place is disconcerting, to say the least.

And all the bodies. They were not the trim, fluid bodies of Cecilia. And they were certainly not the fine-muscled bodies of the runner. Is not one of the purposes of exercise to acquire a physique that looks as though it receives attention?

"It's in the mind, the spirit," Cecilia said of her beloved yoga. "Do what you love. The body will follow."

And what does that notion have to do with Doug? How involved is her spirit with this guy, and has her body followed?

I hadn't seen Cecilia since that September day, and now that it was nearing the holidays, I thought about her more and more. Continuously. In fact, that might be what it meant to "obsess."

I closed my eyes at night and saw her. When she'd taught kindergarten and was "Mrs. Grove." She'd set up a Christmas tree in her classroom where the students hung their awkward, sparkling paper ornaments, heavy with excesses of glitter and glue. Some branches nearly resembled a weeping willow's, drooping under the weight of especially ponderous ornaments. The first year we were married, I stopped by her school on my lunch hour to surprise her. All those children, little hands joined, singing in a circle game, and looking up at Mrs. Grove in adoration. I was a hero simply because I was her husband.

I could never forget how Cecilia's eyes shone, her lit face radiant like the tree resplendent in the corner of the room, her pink lips forming an open smile of surprise when she spotted me in the doorway with my offering of gingerbread man cookies.

"You're the best," she whispered, admiring the cookies decorated with red shoestring licorice and white frosting. She showed the cookies to her class. "Look what Mr. Grove brought us." The children responded with "oohs" and "ahhs," and I knew my status in their eyes had risen all the higher. My eyes grew wet. As I left, the doorway blurred and I smacked into the doorframe. A child giggled, most likely thinking I was only clowning.

Cecilia later said she wished I'd stayed for snack time. I'd tried to imagine myself, a giant in that world, drinking from a tiny carton of milk, goofy with sentimentality, my weepy eyes diluting the children's hero worship. I'd made the right decision to leave when I did.

I was never able to bring myself to return to the classroom. I knew I would let Cecilia down with my cloddish behavior. I was too clumsy in expression; I didn't know how to accept adulation I didn't deserve. Okay: children frightened the hell out of me.

Her students performed a short play each Christmas, at the end of which, orchestrated by the principal, a student presented Cecilia a bouquet of red roses. She showed me the photos. Inevitably, the cherubic students wore white ruffled pinafores, red velvet dresses, a green plaid bow tie, and the pictures had the aesthetic appeal upon which greeting cards could have capitalized. However, unbeknownst to Cecilia, sometimes I stopped at the school and listened from the hallway to the goings-on inside her room. During particularly rambunctious games, I braved moving closer to where I could glimpse the activities. I always experienced a surge of intense emotion when I saw her patting this child or praising that one. I took the emotional swell to be love. And pride, yes, that, too.

I didn't know exactly what I feared about a mass of little bodies jumbling over the carpeting. I only knew that I didn't belong. But when Cecilia began to tell me that *she* had come to feel out of place, I was confounded. Cecilia? She, who mixed and set out the little pots of primary colored paints and took up the paintbrushes without hesitation. Who moved with ease in the children's games, skipped with delight or flapped her arms like wings. Who sang with the high pitch of a child herself, chirruping lyrics off-key with conviction and purity.

"It no longer means the same to me," she said. "I don't feel like 'Mrs. Grove' anymore. Did I ever? Who is—who *was* she?" She sighed. "I'm tired of feeling like the world is 'out there' and I don't know anything about it other than from the translated perspective of the five-year-old mind."

The trouble was, Cecilia saved this explanation for after she'd already made up her mind to quit her job. How could she not have realized I would comprehend the desire to see the world through a different lens? I knew the suffering she experienced. I understood her craving. I should have said: You think I don't get it, dearest. But think how it must be for me. In the stores, the person ahead of me at the checkout holding out plastic—imagine what goes through my head. Constantly people whipping cards out of their wallets without a care, and when the cashier asks, *put this on your charge?* I hum so I can't hear the response. I want to say to the customer, *Look, do you really need that bracelet? Do you know how much that piece of costume jewelry will really cost you in the long run?* You have never seen people fall apart in front of you when they hear the true state of their financial affairs—I'd rather tell a five-year-old a story any day.

I'd done a lot of that kind of thinking, about the hazards of one's career. The police officer must see every individual as a potential law-breaker, the capacity latent inside like an apple with its core; the librarian must dread rainy nights, teenaged patrons with bubblegum, greasy restaurant tables. The list for portentous disaster was endless. The inability to escape noticing the capriciousness of calamity looming in the world was just another hazard of one's occupation that varied only according to the nature of one's job.

So, indeed, I understood Cecilia's discontent, though perhaps I was too cavalier, once she explained. I admit that I was afraid. I'd felt we worked together. We had a sound financial plan: a sensible budget, savings, retirement accounts, investments. This strategy relied on her salary, too. Though I would never find myself in the shoes my clients did, I was concerned. I'd seen people who were otherwise rational react to the ends of relationships in fiscally damaging ways. I suppose it was that apprehension that motivated me to respond as I did to her pronouncement that she was leaving. "You won't get a penny from me," I said.

We had always maintained our own checking accounts. Separated, Cecilia would manage, if she kept her head. With her new job at the music store, she'd keep up the payments for her car. Legally, she could make an issue of that since the car loan was in both our names, but she didn't care to discuss finances.

I suspected she might have to dip into her savings now and again to make ends meet. She knew full well what a mistake that could be. I wondered how she afforded her rent on the apartment above Four Winds Cafe, where recently she'd started singing on certain weekday evenings. Singing! What about her asthma? Perhaps the vocalist position helped, but remembering that voice in the kindergarten classroom, I was surprised anyone would *allow* her to sing, let alone pay her to do it.

The way I found out about her singing was discomforting. "Are you related to the Cecilia Grove, the singer?" asked a new client. "She's fantastic!" the woman bubbled.

"Very talented," her husband added—too enthusiastically. I looked him over in the way I have for letting people know that that's precisely what I'm doing. I raised my eyebrows, just perceptibly enough so that the action was noticeable yet seemed a natural reaction to my thoughts, while my eyes grazed over his expensive tailored shirt.

"That's something we need to discuss," I said. "How much of one's budget should be allotted to entertainment. What do you estimate you...*spend*...at this cafe now?" The correct term was, of course, "waste" but I was careful to employ tact.

Thus, I steered the conversation back on track, but echoing in the back of my mind were the words "very talented." The man had meant *very beautiful*.

The holidays are tricky. I couldn't stop wondering about Cecilia, her funny voice pealing through a room full of strangers, grown-ups, who should be able to discern the difference between joy and intention and genuine musical ability. I wondered if the way she looked at her world now was more pleasing to her than the myopic spirit she'd claimed to possess when we were together. I wondered if she thought of me. Could she ever imagine that I carried with me, like invisible armor, that image of her, radiant as she held up the gingerbread man cookies to her kindergarten class?

Two days before Christmas I ventured to the Four Winds Cafe. Cecilia stood behind the microphone, wearing a multi-colored skirt, diaphanous in the lights. The fabric seductively revealed her legs, encased in dark tights, and I wished she'd worn something else. She hadn't noticed me sitting in the corner. However, the waitress was quite attentive, and I ordered another beer, one over my two-beer limit. It was almost Christmas, I excused myself. When I'd been in high school, my older brother Jeffrey used to say, "It's Christmas Eve. You can do anything."

Then one Christmas Eve, Jeffrey died. He'd been home from college on break, months away from graduation. Driving home from a party, he lost control of his jeep on a strip of black ice and rolled down a ravine, killing not only himself, but his girlfriend and the unborn child she carried. No one in the family had known about the baby—the "fetus"—I corrected myself. We'd been a family who loved babies. I always thought that Cecilia and I would have at least one; our financial plan allowed for two. Meanwhile, my parents too had both passed away, peaceably but grandchild-less.

But it was not Christmas Eve, and I would make this my last beer. I pinched the bridge of my nose until my eyes stopped smarting.

Doug sat at the front table directly center stage with two other mangy-looking types. At first, in the dimly lit room, it appeared that his companions were both men, but one was actually a very skinny girl with hair that matched her boyfriend's. They held hands and bent their heads to one another, talking into each other's hair.

Cecilia sang on—another folk tune I didn't know—and evidently she had taken voice lessons. Her voice was strong and true, and her breath and pacing gave away no indication that was asthmatic. How was she affording everything? That Doug character? At times she seemed to sing exclusively to him. "Baby, it's cold outside..."

I considered whether I should attempt to attract her attention, but bitterly I realized that if those pseudo-sixties revival people at the front table were now her type, then I definitely was no longer. I looked down at my brown tweed jacket, oddly foreign in that light, and felt for the calculator inside the breast pocket, its rectangular shape that brought me comfort. It was an ancient gadget I'd found in Jeffrey's things, an usable talisman that Cecilia had once mistakenly put through the wash, in the pocket of an Oxford.

Applause broke out. Cecilia's face flushed, I could see even from my seat. I felt paralyzed, as though if I clapped she would know I was there. While her fans continued to express approval, I slipped out of the café and began the long walk home. Snow had begun to fall again, and a light dusting coated my car in the parking lot beside Four Winds. Perhaps at night's end Cecilia would spot my car there and wonder where I was, how I was spending my evening. Would she wonder if I'd patronized one of the nearby bars? Would she guess that I'd drank more than my limit and had left the car? She would never suspect I'd been in her café, would she?

In the sobering brisk air, I considered that I might need some assistance negotiating the pain of my obsessive thoughts. Tomorrow, when my head was clear, I'd deliberate.

Much changed by New Year's Eve, I, with my determination and purchased ticket for the celebration, returned to The Four Winds. Inside the café, revelers sported shiny, conical party hats, shaking or blowing noisemakers in between songs. While I didn't go so far as to participate in the anticipation so demonstratively, I was nonetheless different. It wasn't merely my appearance, though I wore a new suede shirt that complemented my blue eyes and I did wonder if Cecilia would like my new style.

I intended to get her back, to take her home with me, where she belonged.

Since Christmas I'd searched my heart, my soul. I'd sought out an Episcopalian priest for counsel, and oho! The priest was a *she*. The surprise had a remarkable effect on me, raising my spirits, sparking hope. My usual pessimism abated. Now, this was the sort of transformation Cecilia would appreciate.

Cecilia, Cecilia, we will laugh together in simple delight when I tell you what revelation was delivered me—for *us*—and all in this season of miracles.

I'd been in Martha's counsel every other day. Now I understood that while I would never pretend to understand everything that my beloved wife so needed, I would make her see that I wished to learn. I knew now with utter certainty that was what *I* needed, too.

An epiphany, Cecilia!

And then there was the other miracle.

The day after Christmas it arrived, a clear crystal strung on a leather cord. Wrapped in purple tissue paper sprinkled with silver glitter, the gift waited on my desk when I arrived at the office that morning. No one could explain how the shiny package had gotten there. But the meaning was clear: Cecilia cared.

My hand went to my shirt where the crystal hung inside against my sternum. The precious stone remained astonishingly warm next to my skin despite the cold weather. Had Cecilia known this would be the case? This was only one of the questions I wanted to ask, one of the one-million-and-one questions, but it would have to wait its turn.

The carousers in the café danced wildly, gyrations of hips and booties, hands waving in the air. I thought about dancing right in front of Cecilia, where she undulated on stage, her gypsy skirt an airy bell ringing around her hips. But, sweaty-palmed, I sat back down. Cecilia, without pause, went right into a new song. It was now twelve minutes before midnight.

Sweat trickled down my chest. I imagined the crystal moistening. How to reach Cecilia? The main problem was that she needed to come down off that stage. Surely, she didn't intend to perform straight through to the twelve o'clock mark. I tried to calm myself with the notion that, of course, of course, I could connect with her after twelve. This was no fairy tale. I would not turn into a pumpkin.

I wanted her to see me as I was now: soulful, romantic, playful.

I had to reach her before twelve.

I stood, prepared to plunge forward to the stage. Upon the stage! I was, after all, still her husband. I had every right to claim her attention, and at such a portentous moment.

I stepped forward, my legs weak, I staggered. Was I drunk? No, I was not. Drunk with love!

"Sit down," a person at the table behind me called.

"Sorry!" I retreated to my table and took a gulp of champagne.

Cecilia, song finished, took a low bow, and riotous applause broke out, replete with noisemakers and men whistling through their teeth. Something was about to happen: Cecilia stepped to the mic and held up an elegant hand to interrupt the merriment.

"We've all heard the old tradition. The one that says what you do at midnight on New Year's Eve is what your next year will be full of. So I hope your year to come is full of music and celebration."

Mad cheers from the crowd. Raised glasses.

"I also hope," she continued, "if you're with the one you love"— more cheers, and a buzz started up inside my chest— "that you'll be loving and kissing"—she smiled broadly, there was a stir at the front table— "all the year long!"

The crowd went wild: Doug was on his feet.

He didn't use the steps, but took the stage in an easy bound, and handed one of the champagne flutes he carried to Cecilia. His arm snaked around her waist. She beamed. Her shimmering red hair practically crackled. He held his glass up to her. A drum roll sounded.

The crowd counted down: ten, nine, eight, seven, six, five, four, three...

I couldn't tear my eyes from the two of them entwined in the impossibly bright stage lights—where I'd meant to be. Where I was supposed to be. The lights stabbed my eyes. They were kissing, on stage, for all to see.

Everyone was kissing, glasses clinking.

My shirtfront was damp; it was so hot, I felt I could suffocate. Everything was out of control. Blown apart. Far away, kissy people were busy ants. Sound had grown fuzzy. I was losing my hearing. I *was* suffocating!

A tinny yell burst from my chest, and all those tiny distant faces turned my way.

I saw my hands, my arms, my legs, as I rose from the table, the tips of my new boots on the floor in front of me, one after the other, carrying me, but *I* was not attached: I couldn't feel myself attached to any part of my body.

I made it outside, where I barely noticed clusters of people smoking, tiny clouds hanging before them in the winter night. I leaned onto the brick façade. I tore open my shirt. That didn't help, and, desperate, I stripped the shirt off, tossing it to the ground.

"Hey, buddy, take it easy," someone said. He put his large, leather-covered arms around me, and I collapsed against him. Looking up into his face, I saw nothing of his features, but I would forever remember the outline of a cowboy hat against the gray, which was the night sky.

The physician in the ER said some people think they're in cardiac arrest when an anxiety attack strikes. "Yours was comparatively mild." He stepped out in search of a prescription pad.

I experienced relief, but my pride was crushed. Out in the corridor, Doug insisted to Cecilia that I had been merely seeking attention. Spoiling everyone's celebration. Jealous. His words mortified me. I couldn't have thought up such a scheme even if I'd wanted to.

Cecilia entered the room and sat close to my gurney. She took my hand and in the context of this drama, her holding my hand distressed me. I had to make her understand that the anxiety attack was out of my control, but she shook her head and hushed my explanations. She pointed to the crystal hanging over top of my paper gown. "It's beautiful," she said.

"I haven't thanked you yet."

An odd expression crossed her face. "You think I gave this to you?"

"Of course?"

She shook her head, smiling gently, perhaps ruefully. "But it's lovely that someone did."

She looked quite sad then, and I knew at that moment we were not going to get back together. It was finished.

But I'd been so certain. All the signs had seemed to show that I was headed in the right direction. What I'd thought were signs. First and foremost Martha—a kind and brilliant woman who'd come to my aid, helped me see how much more there was to the world than safety. She'd looked at me with compassion, even admiration the day I'd bawled my eyes out over my poor dead brother, who I hadn't known I'd missed so deeply. I tried to express this to Cecilia, my realizations, though I stumbled through my words, revealing myself to be the clumsy dope I'd feared she'd see in me, back in her classroom. I closed my eyes and pictured the door on my sore, caged heart opening.

She said, "You're on the right path. You are." She squeezed my hand and stood. In her silvery, husky voice, she said, "Happy New Year, Henry."

She walked out the door.

Doug's footsteps joined hers, and they faded down the hall.

And so she would go on, without knowing all my changes that I'd been so desperate for her to know. I was sad. But I wasn't devastated. Why the knowledge didn't hurt more was befuddling, surprising. Martha coached acceptance: perhaps that's what it was.

My fingers sought out the crystal, warm and smooth. I wanted to believe Cecilia about the gift and I also *didn't* want to believe her—I wanted it to be her who'd given it to me.

Maybe not-knowing is the gift, I could imagine Martha saying, her mischievous smile lighting her face.

Jeffrey: You can do anything, brother. Yes, a person can do anything. At any point.

I rose from the gurney and prepared to go, zipping on my jacket that Cecilia had so thoughtfully brought from the café. I stepped into the corridor, calm, ready for home. Ready for January 2, the date circled on my calendar, with *Martha 5:15 pm* written next to it in red marker.

FRIENDLINESS

THIS WHOLE SOCIAL MEDIA thing gets me down. IRL being social isn't a priority of mine. I don't enjoy parties, wedding receptions, holiday get-togethers. But management encourages us to use social media (have a personality but avoid expressing political opinions, and certainly no posts about the company's culture), and a guy in the tech industry nearing fifty years of age can't afford to fall behind. How many friends do you have on Facebook? a coworker asked me the other day in the break room. I've got over four thousand, she said. Her eyes were bright and her mobile upper lip moved over her front teeth, rabbit-like. I told her I hadn't looked at my numbers for a long time, which was true. I'd have to check.

Sixty-two friends, mainly work acquaintances. My wife is my friend. Melanie has hundreds of friends. But I don't think she knows them either. She's even shyer than I am: if we're forced to go to a party, she'll take a glass of wine and sit somewhere in the shadows and observe.

This having friends on Facebook is like being the last kid in class chosen in Farmer in the Dell. On my first day of school, when I joined hands with my classmates to form the big apple pie circle, according to the protocol of the game, Karen Ray pinched the flesh between my thumb and forefinger. The teacher said Karen Ray didn't mean anything by it. Of course the girl meant something!

There are many Karen Rays on Facebook, none of whom I'm friends with. Perhaps she's married now, with a different last name.

I was once friends with my son. He has thousands. He's nothing like me. In fact, that was always his goal: to be nothing like me. He's twenty-five now, outgoing, good-looking, and plays guitar in a death metal band. When we were friends on Facebook, I would like the videos of his band that he posted on his page.

I never knew when he unfriended me. One day it dawned on me that I hadn't noticed any new posts from him. I'm sure that says something about me. I'm glad he's a popular guy. I'm glad he's suc-ceeded. In the middle of the night, when I can't sleep, I secretly go to his page, turn down the volume, click on the videos, and watch him scream into the microphone, light from the screen flickering on the dark living room walls. I can't hear the words, but there is something about that anguish in his howling face.

DEVOTEES

A FTER A LATE DINNER of grilled quail, they lolled on the top of the king-sized bed while the huge flat screen opposite them played *The Razor's Edge*, a movie Camelia had wanted to see so long ago she'd forgotten why. She remembered the book—W. Somerset Maugham was the author—on her mother's bookstand, opening and reading what seemed a dreary epitaph to her teenaged self, and replacing the book on the dusty shelf. Lee, her boyfriend, handled the movie rentals, adding and subtracting films in the queue according to his fluctuating desires. She liked giving him that upper hand, so important to him and so insignificant to her.

The bedroom was warm this autumn night in Savannah, and she was almost sleepy. Her pale legs stretched over the steel-gray duvet. A thick pillow arranged next to the headboard cushioned the knobs of her spine, and her chin rested on her chest, rising with each measure of breath.

Close to her naked thigh, Lee's hand gripped the remote. Attached to that hand his unyielding arm, a barricade. Twilight had faded, the room grown dark. Shadowy light from the screen roamed over his face, the rigid jaw, his proud lip. He took care to remain clean-shaven, for when his whiskers showed, they were silver, and he enjoyed otherwise not looking his age. No one had ever made the embarrassing error of mistaking Lee and Camelia for father and daughter.

Camelia knew how to undo that pride. How to make that jaw go slack, his face prayerful; how to suck the beloved Jesus out of his fall, carry him to redemption. What goes up must come down. So had said a neighborhood boy in her backyard, tossing pinecones in the air to demonstrate. She'd been ten. A chip of pinecone had fallen into his eye, scratching the cornea, and he'd had to wear a patch until it healed.

Lee knew Camelia was looking at him—she knew he knew—but he merely turned up the volume. A burst of gunfire and an explosion. Bill Murray, the actor; World War I, the setting. Something sad but predictable had happened, she gathered from the cynical voices of the soldiers. Ah, they were angry about the fancy ambulance that the Ivy League grads had driven, that the vehicle was blown to bits, the grads blown to bits with it. Bill Murray, playing Larry Darrell, must prove his prescience to the jaded soldiers, show them that though he'd just arrived at the Front, he understood: the swanky vehicle made the Ivy Leaguers a target, risking the lives of everyone in the vicinity. So Bill Murray took a crowbar to the headlights of his own ambulance, bashing in the thick metal panels. Wham, wham, he beat his vehicle to a pulp. The smashing loud, violent, but Larry Darrell never flinched.

The Razor's Edge wasn't a war movie per se, but there was a certain set to Lee's face. She could have run the tips of her fingers over his forearm—she'd discovered a particular sensitivity to his skin there—but knew not to disturb him now. His son had gone to war. To Afghanistan.

They never called it "the war." Lee didn't call Michael his son when he spoke of him, which was rarely.

Growing up, Michael had lived with his mother, Lee's ex-wife. One clear night full of stars, while Camelia and Lee swam in his pool and enjoyed the sprawling deck he'd just had redone, he revealed that he'd expected once Michael was free to leave his mother's house, he'd come live with him. They'd been drinking single malt scotch. The warm water in the pool lapped gently up to her chin, sometimes slipping into her ears so that she might have misheard his words: "The betrayal!" Sitting on the edge of the pool, he'd made that wrenching sound in his throat and kicked his foot hard in the water. Michael had skipped college to go to a war that was not a war.

When Lee had been in college, he'd marched in protest against the Vietnam War, skipping classes and hitchhiking to DC. The marches were more important than Econ 101; they were a civic duty. Camelia's mother had protested that war, too, riding a bus eight hours each way to the Capitol. She'd loved those bus rides. The singing. Dylan and Joan Baez. "Where Have All the Flowers Gone?"

Lee and Camelia's mother may have marched by one another on those streets crowded with protestors. The two hadn't met. No one was eager for such a meeting. Camelia's mother had recently hung a reissue of the famous "Primer" poster, displaying the bright yellow graphic with its message "War is Not Healthy for Children and Other Living Things" on the living room wall of her shabby studio apartment. She'd never seemed to experience a crisis of meaninglessness. An occupational therapist, she still worked, unlike Lee, whose money worked for him—and for Camelia too, who floundered, who had yet to finish a degree. In what, she still didn't know.

Larry Darrell was Bill Murray's first dramatic role, and it wasn't going well. All the reviews had said the movie was a flop, a rotten tomato. "It's his body—it's just always funny; Bill Murray can't *not* be funny," Lee, who always read reviews, had said, an explanation for why he hadn't thought the film to be worthwhile when she'd suggested it.

On the screen, Bill Murray emoted, his face portraying compassion and wisdom: he was home from the war now and *knew* what his peers couldn't possibly. They simply weren't capable, he understood.

Lee didn't know Michael was actually home now. Camelia talked with Michael on the phone, something else Lee didn't know. Michael was undergoing rites to become a Zen priest. He'd described a ceremony that involved a monk placing a coil of incense on the inside of his arm and another monk lighting it. He watched the flame move over his skin.

"Did it hurt?" she'd asked. She'd imagined Michael to have been in a trance of some sort, something faith provided. Was such a faith possible, one that could overtake the body?

"Fuck, yeah," he'd said. "Pain is how you know you're alive."

Camelia's mind went to those chariot parades in seventeenth-century India, where devotees sacrificed themselves under the wheels of the carriages carrying images of Vishnu. She lifted Lee's hand from the bed, removed the remote from his grasp. She brought his old thick hand to her lips. The flesh between his thumb and forefinger was warm and salty. Her teeth sank in.

A yelp. He wrenched his hand away. His hand bashed her across the face. The metallic taste of blood filled her mouth. She smeared her mouth on his.

SEVEN

SHE KEPT ON SMILING, AND HE BEGAN
TO BE AFRAID THAT HE DID NOT KNOW
AS MUCH AS HE THOUGHT HE DID

WEDDING GIFT

TEN DAYS BEFORE THE wedding, out of the blue, on an ordinary Wednesday evening at dinner—roast beef, baked potatoes, canned corn—Donna's father capitulates: "I will walk you down the aisle." He announces this in his way that means he is offering her a gift but that she must not make a big deal out of it. They are supposed to treat this new circumstance as *Of course I will do this thing that any father would do for his daughter he so loves!* While, on another level, *Don't take this for granted, my girl!* For Donna to show surprise or too much enthusiasm would make it seem that he's capable of not being the loving father—she never knew why he'd earlier refused to take part in the ceremony—and then, hurt and offended, he'd have no choice but to rescind, to show her what it would be like for him to be that kind of person. He forks another bit of roast into his mouth.

Donna's eyes don't know exactly where to go. She's a muddle of internal processes: shifting guts, thumping heart. She sees without seeing the meticulously carved squares of meat on her father's plate, the bright shavings of butter melting on his dinner roll. She has to say something. So she accepts as she's learned to do: "Thank you," her voice even, emotion checked.

Her father chews, his jaws rhythmic, precise. Each time he subtracts a piece of roast from his plate, he rearranges the remaining squares as if to obscure the deletion.

Donna picks at the corn on her plate, preparing herself. The kitchen is too warm for this evening in May, the result of having the oven on for the potatoes her father likes regardless of the weather. She finds a casual tone to say, "There's a rehearsal next Friday, the night before. You would need to come to that."

Her father thrusts his fork deep into his baked potato. The brown jacket splits; wafts of steam escape. Industriously, he mashes the fluffy insides with his fork. So white, the potato. Everything so bright. Her yellow yellow corn.

"What's to rehearse?" he says. "Nothing to it."

So he won't attend. It doesn't matter. It's not a typical wedding rehearsal anyhow. You're supposed to have at least a nice dinner party. But after all, there's only Gary and Lisa, Randy's brother and sister, making up the wedding party. "Standing up for us," Randy calls it. Donna's skin feels clammy; she's both sweaty and cold.

"I asked what time is the wedding?"

"Sorry. Nine," Donna says. "A.M." She gives a little laugh. "Of course. A little early, I guess. That's what Reverend Stevens said, anyhow."

He snorts. Donna's face blazes. It isn't early for him. When her alarm clock rings at six, he's already long gone. Sometimes he leaves for work while stars are still in the sky. Placing his napkin beside his plate, he pushes away from the table and goes for the stairs as he does each evening after dinner, up to the bathroom to spruce up. He's proud that he keeps his nails clean and trimmed. Donna has seen for herself how the other movers in the company always have dark half-moons of dirt under their nails.

She starts on the dishes, scraping the food from her plate. Randy thinks she is losing weight to fit into her wedding dress, but the truth is she's simply unable to eat. She imagines she'll get her appetite back once she has her own home and can prepare meals that she'd enjoy—and Randy, too, of course.

But here is her dad, ready to go to Uncle Jim's where, like most nights, he and his brother watch TV until eleven. He stands before the hallway mirror, his damp hair slicked back from his forehead, and watches his clean hands screw his cap into the right position. He turns his head to each side to check that the brim is even. "Never judge a book by its cover," he says.

Who knows what he means this time, dropping his blessed aphorism? The door closes after him and Donna hurries through finishing the dishes. Randy, like her father, is never late. He doesn't like to wait on people.

Seven o'clock, Randy's truck pulls up. He takes off the moment Donna slams her door closed. They're off to the house where they'll live; Randy has been updating the little bungalow his grandfather left him.

She braces herself, fastening the seatbelt. "Only ten days!" she says.

"Yeah," Randy says. He's in a bad mood. He guns the engine, turns up the radio. His palm pounds out the song beat on the steering wheel.

Donna snugs next to him, places her hand on his thigh. "Don't worry. You'll get it done."

Randy shakes his head gloomily. He could use a haircut and his beard needs trimming. Donna doesn't like his goatee but it does make him look more mature, and that's important, he says, in his line of work—construction.

"You will. Look at everything you've accomplished already."

It was just three months ago that Mr. Carter died. They spent a full two weeks cleaning first. The old pack rat had lived alone for years. Mountains of newspapers were stacked alongside the living room walls. Machine parts, broken appliances, and scraps of metal filled the room, and the narrow path of floor leading to the kitchen was grimy and splotched with stains that seemed impossible to remove. In the kitchen, there'd been a dark rectangular patch on the linoleum that, tracing it with the toe of his boot, Randy pronounced, "Car battery."

Now Donna reminds him of all he's achieved: floors refinished, kitchen remodeled with new tile laid, and the bathroom, too; all the plumbing, walk-in closets in the bedroom. "All that in no time."

A hint of pride softens Randy's face. Pulling up next to the bungalow, he ruffles the hair on her head as if she were his puppy.

Sometimes Donna feels like Randy's pet, a faithful companion at the ready. She sits on the floor of the closed-in porch, watching him handle the power saw. He's confident and skilled, and his cuts into two-by-fours are so clean, so true, that no trace of the pencil lines he drew in measurement are visible. Donna wonders what, if anything, she'll be that good at. Her father advises her to stay on at the bakery where she's been working since she was fourteen, though then it was only part time, weekends and summers. After graduation last May, she went to full time. He's fond of some aphorism about there being no shame in good, honest work.

It's not that Donna isn't any good at decorating—the duty she'd finally worked her way up to. It's that, well, this work is not the stuff of dreams, not for her. Her father thinks that makes her a snob. *Do you think you're too good for it?* Her mother had been a housewife all her life, he reminded her.

Her *short* life, Donna would've liked to point out. Though she'd only been three when Alice Livingstone died and can't for sure know who her mother was, Donna still can't help believing that, had her mother lived, eventually she would've wanted to do something more than keep house. Donna doesn't know any mother who stays home all day. Randy's mother, like most, works at the sewing factory. She loves having her own money, her "independence." Mrs. Carter would be glad to put in a word for Donna with management.

But Donna has other ideas. She's looking into courses of study at the nearby branch of the state university. "Whatever you want to do, sugar," Randy has said. He hopes she'll choose a field that brings in lots of money.

Flurries of sawdust settle in soft piles on the floor around her. When there's a break in Randy's sawing, she'll sweep it up. She draws in its pungent aroma, the smell of new. Beginnings, possibilities. Donna finds a pen and paper in her purse, an order form from the bakery, and on the back practices writing *Mrs. Randy Carter*. So unnatural! She wouldn't change her name if she thought she could manage to keep it from her father. He would take it personally if she were to buck tradition. *Why do you always want to rock the boat?* he's demanded.

"Donna Carter," she whispers. So odd. That's the name that will go on her diploma one day. She firms her voice. "Mrs. Donna Carter."

The high-pitched squeal of the saw whirs down. "What?"

"Nothing." She gets to her feet, brushing sawdust from her jeans, and goes for the broom. "Sorry."

Randy bends back to his work and turns on the saw, an irked expression torquing his face.

He's just stressed. She takes the broom to the outline her body marked in the dust.

After rehearsal, holding hands, Randy leads Donna down the church steps. "That wasn't so bad," he says. His laugh sounds like he's letting out a long-held breath. Donna's tense, too—her hand is balled inside Randy's. She removes it from his grip and shakes it out.

"What did you think of the way he kept on us? 'Be on time, be on time.'" She slides into the truck. "That was really getting on my nerves."

"Reverend Stevens is an old fart." Randy starts up the truck and shifts into gear. "Forget about him. What do you want to do?"

"I don't know." Donna chews at a snag in her thumbnail.

Randy pushes her hand away from her mouth. "Quit that. You want to be all beautiful tomorrow, right?"

"Fine. Let's go get a manicure."

Randy laughs, gives the truck some gas. He's always in a hurry. He pulls onto the highway and turns up the radio, starts singing along, loud.

"Hey, come on!" Donna turns down the radio. "I hate that song!"

"I bet I can change your mind about that tune. I think you can come to love it, matter of fact!"

Donna rolls her eyes. "Where are you taking us anyhow?"

Randy just grins.

"Well?"

Randy accelerates. A little thrill zips through Donna—maybe he's planned something special. But if so, he wouldn't have asked where she wanted to go. Or would he? He might have been trying to throw her off track; that was his style. "Where?" she asks.

"Chill, my old lady. My honey bun, my sugar cookie. Don't you know good things come to those who wait?"

Donna laughs but the pet names bug her. "Okay..."—she searches her mind for just the right name—"I don't know...how about *Daddy*?" It pops into her head. "That's what Janis Joplin always said." Randy loves Janis Joplin; last year at the homecoming party, he'd introduced her music to kids who'd never heard of the long-gone singer, including Donna. That night Donna realized she was falling for Randy.

Randy laughs and says he likes that just fine. He gives the truck more gas.

Good things come to those who wait rings through Donna's head. They haven't exactly waited for anything, have they? They're the only couple from school getting married.

Randy turns off the highway and pulls into Springer's campground. "Oh, great!" Donna says.

They got into trouble here once, Harry Springer walking in on them in an old cabin, dilapidated but suiting their purpose. "I've a good mind to call the police," he said, while Donna scrambled under the quilt, adjusting clothing, grateful for darkness. Silhouetted in the doorway, Springer held an unused flashlight in one hand. "Was young once, too," he said, voice gruff to cover softness, and stepped outside to wait for them. "Don't come back," he said when they emerged.

"Thank you, sir," she said, embarrassed about the quilt she carried in her arms. Randy made a derisive noise and Springer shined his flashlight on him. In the old man's expression, she saw that Randy looked familiar to him, that the man was struggling to place him. At twelve years old, Randy and a buddy had been arrested at the campground for breaking into campers and he'd been put on a year's probation of community service, cleaning up trash in Memorial Park Saturday mornings.

Springer said, "You get on your way, mister."

"It's not like we were stealing or anything. You can't rent that shack!"

"Trespassing, Randy?" Donna prompted, and turned to the woods where, at the muddy road's end, the almost-hidden truck waited, the night air rich with the smell of decaying leaves.

Inside the truck, Randy raged. "You didn't have to stick in your two cents."

"You didn't need to use the word 'stealing!' *Just* the word to jog his memory." He drove her home without speaking and barely pecked her goodnight on the cheek before dropping her off, but he knew she was right, Donna was sure of that.

Now, here at Springer's, she says it's a bad idea to get arrested the night before their wedding.

"Relax! It's just one stop on the tour. We're leaving in a sec. First this." He pulls out a cooler from behind the seat and rattles through ice. "Surprise!" He holds up a bottle of champagne.

"Shouldn't this be for special occasions? Like, oh say, a wedding tomorrow?"

"You're not turning into an old nag already?" He pops the bottle open and hands it to her. "You first. To us."

Donna tilts the bottle and drinks.

They take turns, passing the bottle back and forth, and Donna grows used to the fizz tickling her nose.

Randy drives them here and there around town. "The hallowed grounds of our youths," he calls Springer's, the park, the high school. They stop at the playground and chase and grab at each other in the dark. *Slap and tickle*, her father calls it.

Randy drives to the lake, no hallowed spot for Donna, where once Randy swam, naked and high, with Pamela Mason, where he lost his virginity to the older girl. Donna knows the story. Pamela of the long, glossy hair—tall, long-legged, big breasts. Donna can't stop her mind's eye showing the girl's torso emerging from the water, moonlight making her wet body shine. Rumors were that Pamela Mason followed a rock band out of town, some successful group Donna couldn't remember the name of, Pamela part of the entourage now, living in Florida or California, somewhere sunny, far away.

Donna doesn't need or want to hear the story again, especially tonight. Randy, into the Jim Beam now, tells it anyhow, and Donna wonders will he recount the episode after they're married, and if he does, when will he stop? He can't tell the story the rest of their lives, can he?

The next morning Donna oversleeps, her alarm clock never sounding. Maybe she forgot to set it. She flopped into bed like a hooked fish onto a slippery mud bank; that's the last she remembers.

There's no time for a shower, and riding in Lisa's car, the air close and damp, she tries to stop fretting about that. She and Randy can shower together later. Man and wife. Her stomach flip-flops and she puts down the window.

"My hair!" Lisa shrieks. She caps her head with both hands. The car, badly out of alignment, noses toward the line of parked cars in front of the church. Donna screams and Lisa laughs. Lisa pretends to lift both hands from the wheel.

"Knock it off!" Donna's voice is shrill.

Lisa adopts a nonchalant manner as she coasts into the parking lot. "We're here," she singsongs.

Donna leaps out, slamming the door shut hard.

"Grow up!" Lisa's taunt carries across the lot.

It's ten till the hour, and her father hasn't arrived. The anteroom, where Donna sits in an old wicker chair beside the window, holds a peculiar odor of lemon furniture polish, perfume, and must. She forces her mind away from his absence, imagining the brides in this room who came before her, sucking in bellies before the mirror, smoothing stubborn strands of hair, lamenting a sudden snag in the pantyhose—innocuous, unimportant tidbits that except for that one moment don't matter, nothing else ever again quite so clear as the imperative that the bride must look perfect. She's never seen a picture of her mother on her wedding day. The only time she asked her dad if she could see one, he answered in a way that made her understand never to ask again. *There are no pictures.*

She watches a nervous Lisa reapply foundation to hide a new pimple. "You can't tell," Donna reassures her.

Lisa slaps the mirror, her hand leaving an oily smear.

Donna stands, smoothes her skirt. "Get it together," she tells Lisa on her way out of the room.

Nine thirteen, the clock in the vestibule displays. Donna waits in the empty chamber, hands moist, stomach queasy, headache returning, the aspirin she took earlier worn off. She examines her sleeves, a hair's breadth too long, and thinks she should have stitched them to stay under. Her dress overall is too big and she wishes now she'd had it altered.

The doors creak open. It's him.

He wears a three-piece suit, dark green. When he spots her, her father nods at her like he does acquaintances in the aisles of the Save-A-Lot. But he's visibly flustered.

Donna finds herself moving toward him as if under the spell of what perhaps her grown married self will be, and shows him the white carnation, edges tinted blue. "Yours," she says.

He nods his permission and she works to pin the boutonnière to his lapel. His posture is rigid, holding himself still for her. She can't remember ever having stood this close to him. The intimacy: her hands on his jacket, him allowing it. Her fingers tremble. She keeps pushing the pin and finally the fabric gives. The long pin glides through and stabs into her forefinger.

She tears her eyes away from the spot of blood on his lapel, a dark ugly blot beside the flower, ashamed, and sucks her finger. What will he think when he sees it later, she no longer there?

The minister's globe-like head bobs into sight, a metered revelation rising up the basement stairs. He shoe-squeaks across the carpet to shake her father's hand. "I have another wedding at eleven?" he reminds Donna. The eyes behind the lenses of his glasses are cold. "I'll give the organist her cue." His lips stretch briefly into what he must mean to be a smile before he disappears down the steps.

Silent seconds pass long, loud. Her father gazes off over her head, his eyes glazed, him far away somewhere she'll never know. Words come from nowhere Donna knows.

"I don't want to do it."

He takes her hand.

His hand! Skin tough, fingers thick. Warm. Her eyes sting.

"You're just nervous." He leads Donna to the doors where, on the other side, pews hold a handful of waiting people.

The organ music transitions into the wedding march, and her gut clenches. "I have to go to the bathroom!"

His face pales. His hand tightens.

"Daddy!" And Donna is struck with the hilarity of her saying *Daddy*. As if they were any father and daughter—ballgames, sharing a favorite TV show, ordering pizza, raking leaves together. "I don't want to!" How strange her voice sounds, plaintive, child-like; the wail of a little girl who doesn't want to take her medicine.

His thick eyebrows draw together, lacing panic and irritation. "Just nerves!" He releases her hand and pulls her arm through his, how he thinks it's to be done.

Now the doors open, people standing, turned, expectant. He begins, Donna looped to him. They move, the pressure of his arm seeming to burn through her sleeve. Later, in anger, Randy will tell Donna that she and her father looked like automatons, and he'll repeat that frequently when they fight, as if by fighting about this moment—when everything might have turned out differently—the fight itself might change things.

At the altar, Donna's father halts. Everything pauses. He seems to realize the wait is on him. He gives a start. Self-conscious, trembling, he kisses her.

Donna fills with pity. With sorrow. Bile releases an acrid taste in her mouth. "Thank you," comes automatically, an unbidden whisper. "Thank you for everything."

AN INCIDENT WITH
THE BROTHER

THERE HAD BEEN AN incident with the brother. Anna blamed herself. She'd overindulged, and in the bar had done nothing to stop Jonathan when he reached over from his stool and pressed his mouth onto hers. She hadn't pulled away. His hand cupping the back of her head firmly had imprinted itself into her senses: warm, sure. After the startle of the kiss evaporated, she'd begun to return it. She was almost sure that was true. Anna took the blame and Jonathan, her boyfriend's brother, let her.

A couple days later, Anna wrote Jonathan a long letter about the incident, offering theories about why it had happened. Somewhere she'd read such attractions were only natural. After all, siblings were of the same material at the source. *Look at how your mother named you all James and Jonathan and Janet!* she wrote but, on second thought, scratched out. It seemed wrong to bring the mother into this. *Did you know once it was common practice for a man to marry his brother's widow?* After her great-grandfather had been found frozen in a snow bank, where he'd collapsed on his way home from the mine, her great-grandmother had walked eighteen miles through the night to escape just such a fate, marriage to a brother-in-law she detested. But what did that have to do with things—Anna certainly didn't detest Jonathan—and she scribbled out that line, too.

She tore the sheet out from the legal pad, poured a glass of cabernet, and prepared to start over. Light was beginning to fade in the kitchen. The weather had grown warm again. The window was partially open, and a small breeze swept in. Next door, the Christmas lights strung along the eaves on the neighbors' house blinked on. She hadn't hung lights outside since that first year when Phoebe had come home from college, oh, only forever ago. Another lifetime. Was her girl still in New Mexico now, and if so, did they decorate for the holidays? The breeze blew over the back of her neck, raising goose bumps. She should think what to prepare for dinner. James—he'd been away on a business trip up to Atlanta—was due to arrive home from the airport by six. They hadn't made any plans, but likely he'd be expecting something. She poured more wine and filled a clean page of the yellow legal pad, the inked loops of the words sprawling looser as she wrote. Would Jonathan even be able to read the letter?

He would, and he wouldn't be the only one.

James banged in through the door and entered the kitchen, bag in hand, and stopped to kiss the back of her neck. "Your hair looks good up like that." He set down the bag and opened the refrigerator door.

"Bottom shelf," she said.

He took out a beer, unscrewed the cap, and drank. "Ah," he said, and smiled. He pulled out the stool to sit beside her, but she gathered her tablet to take to her desk. "Tired," she said, and gave him a rueful smile. The neighbors' lights blinked changing colors across James's handsome, drawn face.

Not one of the speculations Anna wrote in the letter rang true. She hadn't been attracted to Jonathan. He was thin and anemic-looking, and the ways in which he was like James—often interior, and from within his aloofness, seemingly evaluating—were unappealing. Perhaps in writing the letter she'd actually been seeking his reasons. Why had *he* done it? That kiss: had it been some sort of test? He'd kissed her and when she responded—she felt certain she had—he drew back and pronounced, "You're bad!"

She was bad! She!

At the time, the blurry time—a loud band, light reflecting from the gleaming copper bar top, refracting from the glassware hanging overhead, catching the shiny shaker in the bartender's hand—nothing clear but Jonathan's warm hand gripping her head, mouth on hers, she took *You're bad!* to mean that good kind of bad. The teasing lilt in his voice. She was bad-exciting. Bad-sexy.

They went out into the parking lot, into the chilly Tallahassee night air—there'd been a cold front and they'd been dancing in light sweaters, hers a loose-fitting green silk. Dressing earlier, there'd been the conundrum of what to wear, her mind fast forwarding to what pieces of her wardrobe she'd be able to keep, her breast still too swollen for the surgeon to know how misshapen the procedure would leave her. So the baggy sweater, a little skirt with snug black tights, her new boots. The boots James had bought when they'd gone away to the mountains. "I guess they're impractical," she'd said when she spotted the sleek leather boots in the shop window. They'd driven into the quaint town for more supplies, as they jokingly called their errand: alcohol was mainly what they were after, wine for her, scotch for James. It was only natural to unwind when on vacation, was the tacit understanding.

"I'm getting those boots for you," he said. "We won't always live down there."

James wanted out of the South, with its dearth of distinct seasons and stifling politics opined in drawling voices. He'd moved from Providence for his job, financial analysis for a corporation that had recently begun demanding that he travel to seminars to acquire more particular certifications, and with each return home, he seemed less content, the contrast of other cities highlighting the deficiencies of life in Tallahassee.

In the bar, Jonathan said of Anna's boots, "They're different. But cool. I like them."

She said, "Your brother has good taste."

"James picked these out?" Jonathan sounded disbelieving.

Anna thought for a moment. "Not exactly, I suppose. He just paid for them."

The boots had been lovely to dance in. And in the parking lot, they gave her firmer footing, as did Jonathan's arm under her arm. The air would have been cold on her damp, sweaty nape, but she didn't feel it. Overhead, a bulbous moon lit planks of skittering clouds in the blue-black sky, and she exclaimed over the dramatic sight to Jonathan, who laughed. She let herself be enraptured, grateful, too, for the anesthesia of the drink that helped to dull the pain of her breast, the agony that thudded like a bass line under the thin chorus of pain medication. Otherwise, the wound salted with sweat would have been excruciating. Against doctor's orders to avoid exercise, she'd danced and danced with Jonathan, who, unlike James, wasn't a good dancer.

She'd met James at a dance at the neighborhood park one summer evening. She and Phoebe, home from college for the summer, had drifted over to the park after dinner, her daughter wrinkling her nose at the plastic cup of beer Anna bought at the concession stand. Phoebe was beginning her spiritual quest in earnest then and saw intoxication as an impediment. The little block-long park was packed with enthusiastic dancers, shaking it up on the grass while the musicians blew their horns and Latin rhythms pulsed the air. James appeared, extracting himself from the crowd, and beckoned for her to join him. Phoebe gave her an encouraging push forward.

They were all happy that night.

Phoebe had genuinely liked James, and how could that not have made somber James all the more appealing? The handful of men Anna had dated over the years—she and Phoebe's father had never married; he'd never been involved with Phoebe, who seemed to have made her peace with that early on—had rarely met with Phoebe's approval. Anna had no idea exactly why Phoebe had so liked him, and now that Phoebe was out of contact, perhaps she would never know.

We never go dancing anymore—a common complaint among couples who'd been together a while. She and James hadn't gone to the park dances in the three years they'd been together. But James loved to dance, he'd said. His enjoyment was obvious that night, and she'd seen no hint of his intensely somber reserve in the rhythmic stamp of his feet, the exuberant swing of his arms. Yet he'd lost his interest in dancing, while his brooding side seemed to magnify. It was as if he'd become someone else entirely. He insisted, "No one stays the same."

She'd become someone different, too. A section of her left breast had been removed. When you have a lump in your breast, even before you know what it might mean, you begin blaming yourself. Drinking tap water. Drinking wine. Some way that she hadn't taken care of herself, had grown slack or not paid enough attention. There were the irrational thoughts, too: too much sex, too little, the wrong partners. "We're going in," the surgeon had said on the phone, explaining that the lab results were inconclusive. An excisional biopsy. "Why leave it in there when we don't know what it is?" He said, "In and out," and handed the phone over to his secretary for scheduling, details, instructions.

Even before the biopsy, from the moment the surgeon made the determination, James began to avoid her: late hours at work, a big game on TV at the sports bar with friends. Each morning he was gone before she arose for work, those last few days in the office before she went on medical leave, though once upon a time he'd enjoyed showering with her first thing in the day. He wouldn't make love with her. Perhaps he was afraid, feared taking pleasure in her body while knowing, as she did, that a treasonous mass lay within the pocket of her unbreached breast. Perhaps the best he could do for her, or for himself, was to avoid active demonstrations of loving the beauty of her so as to lessen the later hurt of her not-beautiful, potentially grotesque appearance. He may have feared betraying a repulsion already in the making. Or maybe his attraction to her had already diminished; he'd grown dissatisfied, and now the surgery made him feel trapped.

Still, she thought James would come around. Before he left on his trip to Atlanta, he'd break down. He'd understand that she needed reassurance, she needed to know that the wounded breast didn't deter him. She was almost desperate for his attention to her physical being. But even that last day, James focused on packing his suitcase as if it were some complicated strategy to execute and notate for future purposes. She couldn't be sure but thought he might have left for the airport early.

Later, she would learn from James's sister that he'd asked his younger brother to look out for Anna while he was away. "He was concerned about your stability," Janet proclaimed. In that phone call Anna would also learn the family viewed her as a seductress, one who could not help but to betray James, even with his own brother. No one would seem to consider James's request of Jonathan an abdication of responsibility.

In the parking lot, under the engorged moon, Jonathan had steered Anna to her car, his arm around her waist as he unlocked the door. He set her in the passenger seat and under those magnificent skies drove them home, to her home with James who was in Atlanta, and they went inside, and she found herself on her bed with Jonathan. Astonished that he had simply placed her there, and was beside her there, on the downy comforter, the stacks of soft pillows wreathing her head.

They shouldn't be there.

She led him to the den. At least she'd been capable of that.

The den where, after James had brought Anna home from the hospital, Jonathan had sat in the big armchair in front of the window, his face blanching when, as James helped to settle her onto the couch, her shirt slid away from her bandaged chest. Shaken by the uncontrollable nature of the pain, she'd winced. The immense force of it, its involuntary sounds. That was her? Making that noise? Jonathan's white face turned away. "I'm fine," she reassured him.

His eyes didn't return to hers, and he spoke to James as if he hadn't heard her. "Let me know if I can do anything," he said. He rose from his chair.

James looked exasperated. "You just got here!"

Jonathan moved toward the doorway. "Mandy'll be home." His girlfriend. Mandy was only Phoebe's age, too young for Jonathan, in his thirties, and certainly too young to be living with a man—in particular this boy-man who'd followed his brother to Tallahassee, though his job as a cashier in the health food store was one he could work anywhere. Surely Mandy's mother couldn't know that her child lived with him. But that was another mother's problem. Anna had worries enough of her own with Phoebe, who, after dropping out of school for the third time, had moved to an intentional community in New Mexico. When Anna hadn't been able to reach Phoebe to tell her about the surgery, she'd been relieved and sad and glad and anxious—what if something went badly wrong? Phoebe, who'd once wanted to practice midwifery, believed strongly that unresolved emotions played a role in the development of disease; she'd once told

Anna that there was a correlation between stored emotional toxicity and the locations in the body where cancers took up residence. Missing Phoebe was pain that coursed through Anna; if her daughter's hypothesis were correct, the inside of Anna's entire body was ailing.

She said, "Say hello to Mandy for us."

James followed Jonathan out to the kitchen, where the two exchanged words she couldn't make out. She heard Jonathan say, "I'll do what I can," and the curtains billowed away from the window in the den, indicating James had shut the back door after his brother. What could Jonathan, who was now afraid to even meet her eyes, do?

James returned with a glass of water and two white tablets on his outstretched hand. Anna swallowed the pills and rested her head against the pillows, anticipating the sweet bye-and-bye, the watery sun on the other side of the curtained window wavering as she waited.

James must have thought Jonathan could do something. Janet's words: "He asked him to look after you!"

She'd had the presence of mind to lead Jonathan from their bedroom into the den, where he pressed himself next to her on the couch. Her eyes fell on the photo on the coffee table, the old cheap metal frame. Awkwardly, she leaned forward and showed the picture to him. "My brother."

Jonathan's voice was sulky, unsure. "He looks cool," he said.

"He's not."

A picture taken about twenty years ago, maybe longer. Handsome Will, tanned and slim, a challenge in his gaze. Who'd taken the picture, she had no idea. Searching through a box of papers for a copy of her living will before the surgery, she'd found the photo and kept it out. Who knew why? James hadn't had much to say about it. He'd never had much to say about her brother, other than "That bastard," when she'd first told him about Will forcing himself on her one scary night when she was ten, how she'd had to fight him to get free, how she and her brother had never spoken a word about it. No one had; she'd only ever told James.

Jonathan took the photo from her hands and put it on the table. "Come here," he said, and positioned her so that they lay beside one another. He placed his hand on her crotch and clasped decisively. A fizz of astonishment rose in her—faraway, but there. The shock got through.

That stayed with her, too: how with that directness, he was unlike his brother.

He moved on top of her, flattening her into the cushions, crushing her breast. She screamed. His head jerked back and he pulled himself, the maneuver grinding his weight into her wound. Agony crashed in on her. She barely registered his hip against hers, his litany, "What am I doing? My brother's woman. What am I doing?" She'd retreated into the purple of her closed eyelids, the pain a room that enclosed her inside.

He cried out her name. *Anna!* over and again. He dragged her back and eventually, she could make herself speak. "What?" the word a loud whisper that hurt.

"Thank you!" he said.

She'd remember that. *Thank you.* Meaning, she supposed, that he was grateful she'd been able to answer him. How could she be sure? How could she know the nature of his gratitude? If she could remember what he'd said next, before finally he let her go into the unconsciousness that was hers to have, she might have better understood. Maybe.

Late the next day, she called Jonathan and insisted that he never tell James what had happened. "It would kill him," she said. Would it

really? Of course not—where had these words come from? *Don't tell.*
Don't tell.

"I think this is something we can keep to ourselves," Jonathan
said. His voice light, and something else. Amused? But that couldn't
be right.

The holidays arrived and they were miserable. Janet was in town with
her toadish husband Brad and timid, pale-faced little boy. When
Janet came visiting from Newark, she expected to stay with James
and Anna, but this time she was at Jonathan's place. "I told her you
weren't up for it just now," James relayed to Anna.

"You could have said 'we'," she said. "*We* are not up for it." James
was just as relieved not to have houseguests; why make her the re-
sponsible party?

Everyone drove over together from Jonathan's apartment and
gathered in the living room. Anna went in the room to greet them.
A sparsely trimmed tree stood in one corner. Decorating the huge
fir—James insisted on a tree as big as the room could hold—had
been too much for her, and he'd been too busy at work. The tree
looked to be too dry already, as if its drooping boughs would begin
shedding needles momentarily. On the nearby window, the shadowy
outline of the wreath hanging outside eerily resembled the silhouette
of a face pressed to the glass. The spirit of holidays long past looking
on, she thought.

"There doesn't appear to be a thing wrong with you!" Janet de-
claimed, catching sight of Anna standing in the doorway. Mandy's
gaze fixed on Anna's chest, concealed under a buttoned cardigan
sweater, much too warm for the evening. Perhaps the remark was
meant to be a compliment. Anna didn't yet know that Mandy had
shared the letter with Janet, that damning document, and that the
two had chosen to condemn her, a wanton femme fatale. She sat

down on the couch where Brad slumped at the other end. Janet and Mandy exchanged a glance.

Near the hearth, James and the little boy poked around at the fire James was attempting to build, while Jonathan, whom she'd not seen since that night, squatted next to his brother. It was too hot for a fire. "We'll have to open the windows," she joked.

"You can take off your sweater," Janet said. She rose from the floor where she had been sitting near the tree, dusted pine needles from her jeans, and exited the room.

James went on with his busywork at the fireplace, and Jonathan, who'd not acknowledged her presence, took the log carrier outside for more wood. Mandy hurried after him. James offered the little boy some instructive trivia. The child knelt beside James, his face beatific in the lights from the tree as he looked up adoringly at his uncle.

Tears stung Anna's eyes. In another, fairer universe, a young Phoebe and a younger James would comprise this holiday scenario, with everything good in the world with them all, all of them awash in the love that was now clotted up inside her with no one to receive it. She got to her feet. "Excuse me. I'm calling it a night."

James swung his head to look at her, his face tightening. "You're tired?" His eyes caught at the shabby fir and the corners of his lips turned down.

"I am, yes." She tilted her head and squinted against the tears. He turned back to the fire, his shoulders rigid. She smiled goodnight at the little boy crouched by the hearth, who, sensing his uncle's displeasure, looked at her worriedly. His face, thin like his uncle's, already held a hint of James's brooding look.

"Sweet dreams," he said, his voice barely more than a whisper.

In her bed, Anna lay and listened to the muffled sounds of James and his family, who were probably drinking cognac. Beer, scotch, wine. They sounded in high cheer. Though she'd always wanted more for them both, her family had been only her and Phoebe. She hoped that Phoebe's holidays were filling her with the sense of connection she'd sought by moving to that community, so far away. She tried not to think that Phoebe hadn't felt connected with her. She tried to hope again that this was simply a phase for Phoebe, one that would take its course.

The tears came despite herself, despite knowing that she was feeling tremendously sorry for herself. There were many in the world who didn't have choices. She was lucky. "Life is what you make it," she'd advised, until Phoebe had declared she never wanted to hear those words again. And no wonder.

Through the walls, the distant voices had raised. Perhaps Phoebe would call on New Year's. If not, Anna would find her. These days you could find anyone, and whatever the cost, Anna would pay it. She carefully laid her hand across her breast and remembered when she was a girl reciting the pledge to the flag in school, how she'd worried about how to place her hand over her heart in public once she had breasts. Even then, it seemed she'd had unformed ideas about how the female body could bring so much trouble, so much sorrow.

James laughed, a rupture of jubilation.

Anna had missed that laugh.

She was going to have it out with him. After Janet took her family back home, Anna wasn't going to spare him the truth. They were going to work it out, one way or another. And if he didn't want her anymore, it was time he owned up to it. Yes, the idea of losing him, whom Phoebe had so liked, was unbearable. I'm sorry, the words rose up from within the well of her.

PERHAPS A KITE

THESE DAYS, ADULTS ARE encouraged to play. Playing makes an adult whimsical, interesting, somehow wiser. Being able to play takes a certain kind of adult. She'd had a friend, an expert in child psychology, who spoke of becoming a different person when she put on a hat, which she liked to do on weekends, going to events like concerts. At the time, she'd been appalled at her friend's behavior. She saw now that she'd had a need to control who she was. If another person had stepped out from within her, who could say what would happen?

Recently, she bought a Spirograph set, remembering from her youth the colorful plastic gears pinned close together onto the paper so that their teeth engaged; the pen traced geometric designs often quite intricate, depending on how long a person stayed with it. This toy seemed like something she could enjoy. But something pressing always arose—some deadline-driven task easily enough forgotten later—and she'd eventually placed the Spirograph box into the cupboard in her home office unopened, along with the package of variously colored pens.

How long can pens keep before drying out? She knew that if she were to open the package and find the pens unusable, she would feel keenly disappointed in herself. Wasting money on ideas for self-improvement. She's managed to cure herself of reading such books, though the volumes still ranged over the shelves of her office, titles unread. Only to graduate to other modes and methods, like toys, for example. Experiences. She was always letting her husband talk her into taking expensive trips to the coast, where she would drag her work—manuscripts to edit, a stack of books she must get read. Also a range of clothing in her bag for long walks on the sand or through the fern-filled ancient redwoods. Her husband emphasized the importance of taking downtime—he knew when she was overwhelmed with stress and no longer productive.

She couldn't afford to be unproductive, that was true, and so off she went on the excursions, where, once there at the inn, she lay on the bed working and trying not to absorb his impatience. He liked to walk. He loved the water. He liked to walk by the water for long times—but with her by his side. Eventually, he would accede to going himself so that she could finish her work, but once he left the room, unable to dismiss the image of his tense, unhappy face from her mind, she would feel like a spoilsport and help herself to a glass of wine. One of her rules was to avoid working while drinking, a practical, necessary rule.

She would look out the broad picture window—the rooms they stayed in always walled by expanses of glass—and would watch the ocean, the changing light in the sky. The treetops moved in the wind on the other side of the cove, telegraphing some uncertain message. She lay on the bed, feelings of inadequacy spreading through her, and imagined her husband in the cooling air, how handsome his back looked as he trudged along the coastline, alone, hands thrust in the pockets of his jacket, a cap on his head to shield his aging face from the sun. She'd always been a disappointment, sang the wine in her blood, and she uselessly poured more to drown out that tune. Perhaps a kite; wouldn't her husband like to fly kites with her on the beach?

LOVE CARNIVAL

They were making dinner together in their galley kitchen. Set over the sink, the one window in the long room displayed the Japanese maple in the backyard, a silhouette in the setting sun. Overhead spotlights lit their work, preparations for vegetable soup—they liked light dinners—and created a reflection of him superimposed over the silhouette so that his head on the glass looked leonine with a mane of leaves. A good-looking man, he appeared vital and virile at age forty-nine, though lately she'd noticed he shed chest hairs in the bedclothes, occasionally on the white bathroom tile floor. The stray curled hairs filled her with melancholy.

Music played in the background, the plaintive notes of Yoram Lachish's jazz oboe rising and falling. Her mind drifted as she chopped carrots. He talked.

She loved that tree despite how its leaves littered the patio in the fall. Already she'd seen a scattering of furled brown leaves over the flagstone, just this morning. She wanted summer to stay. They'd hardly had time to enjoy the season, with its long evenings of light.

Thin disks of carrots accumulated on the cutting board before her. It always took him some time to accomplish his part of the preparations. It was difficult for him to mince garlic and talk at the same time.

Women were the ones adept at domestic tasks. Housekeeping was simply second nature. Once she'd heard a famous poet say in an interview that she wrote her poems in her head while she washed dishes or folded laundry. The poet had lived on a farm and raised several children. She'd founded a prestigious writing program and published several volumes of poetry, books distinguished by important literary prizes. The mind was free to create while the tasks completed themselves, the poet said.

The pile of chopped onion before her was too large. She'd absent-mindedly cut more than needed. Now she would have to set aside the extra or increase the amounts of the other ingredients—the carrots, the celery, and the olive oil, in which the vegetables would sauté, along with the garlic that her husband was still mincing. She didn't want to suggest he mince more garlic. He would want to know why and the answer would lead to a debate on the merits of cooking more than what the recipe called for.

He liked precision. He preferred to adhere closely to a recipe. She rarely followed such directions. She'd been cooking since she was ten years old. She possessed an understanding of the principles, the alchemy of combining divergent ingredients.

As well, to make the request now, she'd have to interrupt him. He was in the middle of explaining the plot of the novel he was listening to during his commute to work. He didn't like to be interrupted. His mother had always interrupted him and in such a way that made him understand that she hadn't listened to a word he'd said. Consequently, he carried large measures of hurt and resentment, so that now his need to occupy the floor when speaking was absolute.

On the other hand, he constantly interrupted her, his wife, his partner, his lover (wasn't she?). She'd wearied of his disrespectful habit and had begun pointing out his interruptions—when she remembered. Perhaps her inconsistency was the problem. Each time she did, he pretended disbelief. Or perhaps he really was surprised, as if her words were of such little consequence that he hadn't even noticed he'd spoken over her. Which he vigorously denied. His vehemence struck her as particularly egregious, heaped as it was upon the injury of his having cut her off in the first place. And so they argued.

Sometimes to demonstrate to him how it felt to have one's words (her words) devalued, she raised her voice and spoke over his heated protestations. Though, of course, when she did this, her face flushing, a hard sensation in her chest below her windpipe, it wasn't the same at all as what he did. What she was denigrating with her demonstration were merely his hollow words of defensiveness. Something to overlook. Out of love, generosity. What mattered, which he proved time and again didn't to him, was the spontaneous sharing of thoughts, which one (she) imagined the other (him) wanted to be privy to. Or ought to want. As in the way of concern for all facets of their intimacy.

She considered adding the extra onion to the pot. The intensity of its taste might not even be noticeable. But if the onion flavor was too strong for his liking, he wouldn't eat the soup. Already the amount they were making was larger than what they could consume in one meal. She didn't want to see the soup languish in the refrigerator, only to have to eventually throw it away, remorseful about the waste. Wordlessly, she pushed the extra onions aside.

He paused in his story and waved his hand over the minced garlic. Was the amount correct, he wanted to know without asking. But he wouldn't care if she were to say that it wasn't quite enough. She knew from experience he'd argue that he'd used three cloves, exactly as the recipe stipulated, and once again she would have to counter that all garlic cloves were not equal in size.

She thanked him. "Go on with your story," she said, while she took the bottle of extra virgin olive oil from the cabinet. She uncapped the bottle and splashed a quantity of oil over the bottom of the stockpot.

Disapproval spread over his face.

How much oil, he wanted to ask. But he didn't want to start up that old argument again. It was as if she had no conception of repeatable results. Though he'd explained to her many times that it was impossible to reproduce a good-tasting batch of soup, or conversely avoid a poor one, if she didn't know the amounts she dumped together—and *dump* was the right word. She'd just upended the bottle of oil over the pot, not a measuring cup in sight.

Each time he'd asked her to see his perspective, she'd argued that it was scientifically impossible to arrive at the exact same soup. They cooked in a kitchen, not a lab! Factors such as the size of the vegetables would always vary, as would their freshness. And the herbs. "How old was the thyme," she'd said once, screwing her face up in an expression to make him laugh at her corny pun.

She looked charming, his wife of almost twenty years: a few corkscrew curls sprung from the golden hair she'd piled up on her head, her complexion dewy in the humid kitchen. She thought he no longer saw her, had accused him of not really looking, of viewing her through the lens of the past. Another button on her red blouse had opened above her breasts. Perhaps the small button had slipped free from its hole as she'd worked, moving from refrigerator to counter, bending down to retrieve the soup pot from its cabinet and lifting it to the stove top, sifting through drawers, selecting knives. Laying out measuring spoons that were only for appearances' sake, to appease him.

She smiled sweetly. "Come on! Cooking is an art, not science," she said. And he knew that in the back of her mind rattled that old squabble about teaching. Art or science. Early on, when they were new and she was looking for a teaching position, she'd confided to him that she'd replaced B.S. degree on her resume with B.A. But no one seemed to notice. Or care. She did, mightily. He had the sense that she would have preferred to have been caught in her duplicity, relished explaining why teaching was an art, as she'd so often enjoyed philosophizing to him.

The button may not have slipped open. She might have unbuttoned her blouse deliberately, and if so, only a few reasons existed why. One might have been for comfort's sake. Bustling around, she'd grown too warm in the steamy room. Her body temperature always ran high. In bed at nights, she inevitably threw off the covers, sometimes rose and cracked open the window, even in January, so that he woke frigid, fingers fumbling as he struggled to close the window. In the summer, she regularly dispensed with her nightshift. Not that he minded. Pure joy to awaken to the sight of her naked body beside him in the dawn, an almost visible aura seeming to hover over her rosy flesh, her flank smooth under his hand.

She knew how much allure her body held, and so the possibility existed that she'd slyly opened the button for him. Did she mean to entice him here, now? He surveyed the countertops littered with vegetable parings. The dirty orange strings of carrot shavings. One cutting board held an extra pile of chopped onion. Over there, discarded parts of the celery. It never ceased to amaze him how efficient she was in the kitchen. In front of him lay only the papery skins of the garlic cloves. Her skin moist with perspiration.

If he were to go to her now, to press his lips to her exposed cleavage, her damp skin would taste salty—salty and sweet. Her skin always carried a faintly sugary flavor, what he imagined the petals of a rose might taste like, though he'd never sampled a rose, had only heard—from her—that many people enjoyed eating rose petals. In India, Pakistan, Afghanistan, people made syrups and ice creams from rose petals. She'd suggested they might try such a recipe themselves, but he'd said maybe. He could imagine what a mess that would turn out to be, her insistence on ad-libbing when it came to the directions.

He began to clear the space in front of him. It was entirely conceivable that she'd opened that button to lure him. But what was her underlying motive? A ruse to distract him from finishing his story? He rinsed the garlic mincer under warm water. Their counselor, Hilda, had suggested they each identify what she called their "triggers," those issues that set them off, and then deploy strategies to prevent them from heading down the same well-trodden paths of no-win arguments. Hilda meant tactics such as using humor. After all, at work he was known for his quick wit and ability to make people laugh, especially in defusing tension in the boardroom. Board members were always glad to see him.

His wife could only imagine this, of course, since she'd never witnessed it. At home he was parsimonious with his sense of humor. Once upon a time, he'd delighted in making her laugh. She remembered fondly the time they were on vacation, reclining on lounge chairs under a huge striped umbrella on the beach in western Maui, and he'd made her laugh so hard that a couple strolling by glared at her, no doubt thinking her drunk. She'd wiped tears from her face, and he'd thrown back his head and guffawed *Oh, Madam!* And that quip, though in and of itself not funny, had set her off again. She no longer remembered what his original inspiration of hilarity had been. It was a long time ago.

Their early years had been a regular carnival, the heightened state of their pleasure in one another more than enough to buoy their boat through the tunnel of love. They clung to one another while in the dark monsters and ghouls abruptly materialized before them, and the grip of his hand tightened on hers as the sensation of some unnameable creepiness dragged over the skin of their faces. Steadfastly, the mechanical apparatus hidden below the dark water in the channel churned their little vessel forward, and they exited into a daylight that stunned and stung their eyes.

She pushed the sautéing vegetables through the oil in the pot with a wooden spoon. Oh, how she'd loved him! And still did, yes, she did. Easy to admit. She'd never been one to talk herself into believing what she didn't in her heart of hearts. Though, before him, she'd almost been in danger of that very thing she'd seen other girls do, try to convince themselves that a boy was everything they wanted him to be—a bad boy, usually. In her junior year in college, she'd had such a bad boy. He'd driven his motorcycle from town to town to see girlfriends, often on the same night. But even after she discovered that she was one of three, she hadn't broken off the relationship immediately, allowed him to return to her apartment several more times. He'd justified himself by declaring monogamy a societal construct antithetical to the dictates of evolution. But she hadn't believed him: that was the difference.

She'd always been honest with herself and was now. She went to her husband and caressed his forearm, the dark hair under her fingertips the perfect melding of substance and silk. He seemed to grasp the faucet tighter, the muscles under her hand constricting, as if he were dedicated to the trivial task by some larger commanding force.

The moist pressure of her small, capable hand on his arm set off a buzz within him. Her nearness. She smelled of onions—look at all that wasted onion—and also, faintly, of some herb. An array of diminutive glass jars of spices stood on the counter. Short thin stalks of something leafy green rested on a square of paper towel, perhaps oregano—was that the scent?—next to the little stainless steel grinder, a device she'd tied with a red ribbon and tucked into his Xmas stocking a couple of years ago. He'd had some desire then for learning how to cook, really cook, an activity that might countermand the stress of his job. But the grinder infuriated him when he'd tried to use it. The teeth had mangled the parsley before the grinder clogged completely. He'd had to dig the clumps of green free with toothpicks. The mechanism was a gimmick; yet, somehow she—never saying a word—had found it useful.

She leaned in closer to him. Oregano, yes, that was it.

She brought her mouth near his ear.

Pressed next to his arm, she felt the heat of his bicep. His shoulder tensed. A muscle flexed in his neck while she reached to kiss his earlobe. He'd always loved her lips on his earlobes. Hilda had meant that they should be creative. When they felt themselves nearing that dangerous territory of explosive bad will, they were to dive down deep into themselves, dredge the golden pail into the waters of desire. She closed her eyes and breathed him in.

This was what she always did. He'd tried to explain it to Hilda. His wife didn't take him seriously. She didn't listen. She used her sex appeal to unfair advantage, to set him adrift. Once again, he hadn't even finished what he'd had to say! He thought she'd enjoy hearing the intricacies of his novel's plot. Even if not, that was fine: she didn't need to appreciate what he appreciated. But she needed to validate him, his interests. He needed validation. He needed acknowledgment. It wasn't too much to ask. He turned off the water, stepped away from her to dry his hands on a paper towel.

The oil in the pot was smoking. She turned to the stove and flipped on the overhead exhaust fan. The mechanical whir invaded the room.

"Do you want to start over?" she said, her words barely audible.

But he had already left the room.

LAUNDRY

S UN BURNS THE MORNING clean. It will be a long time until dirty night comes around; twelve hours is half a day, half of one rotation of the earth. In science class all those years ago, the boy couldn't keep straight the definitions, confusing rotation with revolution—why shouldn't the planet make it around the sun in a day? He was the kind of boy who slid into his desk seat just as the bell ended, as if he'd stolen third base, grinning at his deft rapidity, alacrity—words neither of us knew then, words only one of us knows now. The boy is dead; that is, the man he became. The day will turn slowly with the accruing details of the searing news, images of the accident: crushed bones, blood darkening the earth, something torn loose. Hushed voices, heat lying heavy on the breathing skin. The air in the bedroom close, the closet holding his worn clothes. Half the turn on the axis until darkness. Each day will have to begin again.

SCHEMATICS

Each night before sleep she tells herself the next day will be different. In the morning she'll go down the hallway, turn the old glass doorknob in her hand—her left, to give her dominant right-handed mind notice—and enter the silent room, window shades drawn, the light opaque and indifferent to her presence. She'll sit in the solid oak chair, roll it forward on brass caster wheels to the desk, place her hands on the desktop that holds texts, papers, a canister of pens, the desiccated philodendron, its heart leaves brown and rigid. His laptop is set to the side, a film of dust on its closed lid. He's in the particles she breathes in this study, his epithelial cells, the thirty thousand scales of skin that had flaked off his body per minute. Dust, those bits of a self shed. The science of sadness, oh there are theories. Therapies, drugs. No one really knows anything, he used to say cheerfully, glad to arrive home after a lengthy conference—all those weighty papers presented, the heady conversations and disquietudes, networking over meals of lamb and vegetarian options. He loved this belief of his, the dismissal, the mystery: *no one knows.* The pathways of her brain cells remember his words. Recall his expressions: a raised eyebrow, how his lips turned down when he smiled. His gestures: arms raised, hands spread as if to allow sunlight to pool in the palms. The gentle way he placed a hand on her lower back when they stood together at a party, the not so gentle way he grasped her hips, pressing himself to her on the bed. So go her neurons, making plans for another tomorrow, one that she must believe will come.

Nearly one hundred billion neurons exist in the adult brain—the number of ways to connect all the cells much higher, higher even than the number of atoms in the universe. No one cell in charge of a thought or a behavior. The mind the collective activity of the neurons networked together. If this is the case, out of all the possible combinations of thoughts and behaviors, why does she stay stuck in sorrow? Why must the mind create a pattern like a snare?

~EIGHT~

HOW EVER DID YOU GET LOST ON THIS
BIG SWIFT RIVER, AND HOW EVER
DID YOU DRIFT SO FAR INTO
THE GREAT WIDE WORLD

THE RADIO PLAYED A SONG

S HE'D NEVER MEANT TO have a baby. The baby's father spent his days at a trade school and his nights ostensibly studying on campus. The baby spent most days and nights sleeping, a tiny pink package curled in a white bassinet, or more often in her mother's lap. She, the mother—she had to get used to knowing this was who she was now—spent her days and nights feeling guilty because she hadn't wanted a baby. Not when there was a whole world out there that she knew nothing about, and in this old house in the middle of nowhere, herself whom she knew so little about.

Nights were lonely. She was alone with the baby. She sat by the window holding the sleeping baby and staring out at the pink haze, sodium vapor swaddling the city faraway, the city that held a school where her husband studied. And more.

The radio played a song: *life is what happens while you're making other plans,* and she took consolation in the lyrics. She stroked the fine blonde hair of the baby, whose head fit in the cup of her hand, and fervently hoped that when the baby was eighteen she would live her own plans before becoming a mother. That the baby wouldn't ever know how hard it had been for her mother to stay in the rocking chair alone in the house while wanting to be out in the ruby darkness of night. The mystery of what night held, at the very least a father, most likely in a bar, perhaps complaining to someone beautiful.

The radio played, drawing her heart from her chest. She sang along, thinking even that she sounded good. But the baby stirred and nuzzled her breast as if to remind her mother what her heart was for. She stopped singing. She rocked the tiny girl back to sleep.

FOR UNTROUBLED REST

WHEN MY DAUGHTER WAS a toddler, she often slept with me at night. This was in the days before the trendy co-sleeping of parents and children and the camps of adults who in polarity argued the wisdom of the practice. Her warm body, with its heated musky scent, felt unbearably precious. The nape of her damp neck smelled like grass and twigs. To kiss the top of her head covered in fine shiny hair was to taste the metallic tang of river water. She sighed in her sleep and sometimes a few words rode on her breath that I made every desperate effort to decipher. Once I understood her to say *turtleneck*. She shuddered, her eyelids flickered open, and her eyes glazed with sleep focused on my face for a moment before they closed. Her eyelashes were thick dark crescents on her cheeks, the image so beautiful that I seared it into my brain for when I would need it. She nuzzled her head under my chin and wrapped her tiny arm around me. She'd had a nightmare, I believed, feeling the pace of her birdlike heartbeat slow to normal. I blew softly over the crown of her head, ruffling the wispy brown hair, to soothe her back to sleep. How much power I believed I had then to affect my daughter's very self.

RUST

OUTSIDE THE CAFÉ WHERE they'd eaten lunch, he decisively turned to her and asked what color were her daughter's eyes—her daughter was so observant, it was important to know what her eyes looked like. Her stomach tightened inside her dress, thin fabric wafting in the breeze. So he believed everything she'd said about her daughter, all the stories she'd told. He was interested in the girl he'd never seen.

A smell rose from the stagnant river, like laundry detergent, sickly sweet cherry Jell-O, rusting pipes. The pipes of her had rusted long ago, that was how she explained her lack of children. Like most things in life, it wasn't her fault but she blamed herself nevertheless. She'd always been daring, taking risks that others wouldn't. Even lately, she drank unfiltered water in crumbling cities in the Rust Belt where she also walked the streets at night alone, a large, expensive leather purse hanging from her shoulder.

The wind shifted and the odors died as if they'd never been. He placed his warm hand on her chilly arm, and she could tell he wanted her to invite him over, to the lovely little teal-green cottage at the end of the beach that she'd told him so much about, where lived, too, a white cat, the blue parakeet with a yellow breast, her girl of seven. She liked stories of colorful harmony. If you can tell any story—and we all tell stories—why not tell one that pleases you?

He rubbed the heel of his hand over her arm, raising the fine hairs to stand golden in the light. She thought of all the efforts made to save the charismatic species while the unpopular creatures, like the obscure fairy shrimp that did nothing really but lie in the mud, were ignored. She thanked him for lunch and imagined as she crossed the parking lot to her truck a daughter looking out the window at home, waiting for her arrival, the crunch of her truck tires pulling up over the broken-shelled drive beside the cottage. She imagined the heartbreaking slope of the girl's nose, the gaps in her smile from her missing baby teeth.

HOLE IN THE ICE

As soon as she walked out of the house, the giddy night air filled her lungs, so mirthful she could barely breathe as she slipped under shadows of elms spread over the sidewalk, street lamps dotting the way. Behind her, one such street lamp stood outside her ten-year-old daughter's bedroom window. She'd often caught the girl sitting on top of the hard radiator beneath the window with her book, reading by that light, when the child was supposed to be sleeping. Reading was okay, it was okay! She herself loved mysteries, Erle Gardner whose series about Perry Mason had been made into a TV show. The show a respite, something to look forward to in that household. *Hold*—yes, the house had a hold on her. A death grip. She'd stopped going upstairs at night to check on the girl. Let her read.

Those dark shadows under the child's eyes on the pale skin. She knew what others must think, but she wasn't going to think about that now. *Don't think about that now!* She was free. She wasn't going back this time, no she was not. She hurried ahead to the next block. The air was cool and dank, an iron smell to it. Maybe that smell was snow; every year it snowed earlier. Snow on the girl's birthday in two weeks, most likely. Someone would supply the cupcakes. That's how it worked: people filled in, doing what they should have done all along. Alex Reed says he's a good father. He's so good, let him provide his girl's cupcakes, let him make her a party.

She reached the end of the street, fiery thoughts burning her brain, and waited in the shadows, catching her breath. Any moment a car would come along. Any moment now. Was it, or wasn't it too late to keep going? To turn back? She felt a shiver in her brain, her mind cooling, thoughts thickening, slowing, clotting. When she was a girl. She'd been a girl. One evening falling into a frigid pond at the end of town where she wasn't supposed to be—she'd had no skates, didn't know how to skate; no one in her house had known she was missing. Someone's father had pulled her up through the hole in the ice by her hair, breathed life back into her, his mouth sealed to hers. She wanted that now.

Any moment the car would come along. If the shadows of the elms had lengthened, that was imperceptible. A car was coming.

SENSORY IMPRINT
(ANOTHER FAILING)

S ENSORY IMPRINT, MY GROWN daughter says on the phone, and asks me to send her my sleep shift fresh from the bed when I awake one morning. To pack it tight, and please, soon, don't delay. Touched, bemused, I comply immediately the next morning, having selected my best nightgown to wear to bed and sleeping little, waiting for the sun to rise. Weeks after mailing, fearful, I have to ask if she's received the nightshirt. On the phone, she cries softly: my smell did not reach her.

AN ANCIENT TRADE

S INCE ANCIENT TIMES, THE gem amber has been cherished for its warm glow, its beauty and individuality.

She'd always listened to her daughter's dreams from the time her girl could speak them until the time her daughter, a woman in her thirties, stopped speaking to her.

The classical names for amber, Latin *electrum* and Ancient Greek ηλεκτρον (ēlektron), are connected to a term ηλεκτορ (ēlektōr) meaning "beaming Sun"; it's said that the ancient Greeks discovered amber's ability to produce static electricity through friction and called it *ēlektron*—electron—hence the modern word "electricity."

One late afternoon before their estrangement, while talking on the phone with her daughter as they frequently did—sometimes even a couple times a day (which could dismay her when she had many tasks to accomplish, yet knew that to end the call, no matter how gently she tried to do so, before her daughter was ready would be to risk her girl's hurt)—it had deeply surprised her to hear her daughter say that they'd always had a troubled relationship.

Thousands of years ago, this important raw material, amber—"the gold of the north"—was transported from the coasts of the North

Sea and Baltic Sea overland (in part by way of rivers) to the Mediterranean; this ancient trade route was the Amber Road, and no doubt lives were lost along the way.

Sometimes she'd reminded her husband (who wasn't the girl's father but who had come into her daughter's life when the girl was away at college) of the first "dirty" joke her girl had told (around age twelve), but though she'd repeated the anecdote over the years, today she could only remember that the joke was about a preacher eating dinner with his family who exasperatedly delivered the line, *pass the damn ham*; yet still she remembered how her girl's face had shone, and how hard they'd laughed together, tacitly acknowledging the girl's delight at getting away with using *damn* (had belted the line out with gusto); always her husband kindly listened and smiled, and she knew that made her lucky; she was lucky so couldn't she drop her need for validation of this moment that she and her daughter had shared?

To trade amber with Scandinavia, the Phoenicians, the prehistoric world's greatest sailors and navigators, dared to venture out of the Mediterranean into the Atlantic Ocean.

She'd always believed her daughter when the girl said she was difficult: she hadn't been the best mother, of that she was sure, and could provide a list (and had) of her wrongdoings (asking her girl's forgiveness and falsely believing she'd received it); there'd been so many phone calls (thousands!) without harsh words, until that one when she'd objected to her daughter's assessment of her and her girl hung up the phone on her for what appeared to be the last time.

The Phoenicians, called as such—by Homer—"purple men"—because of their famous murex dye, were enigmatic lords of the sea, who spread literacy throughout the Aegean region with their renowned twenty-two-letter alphabet.

She'd always thought her daughter might become a well-known writer, so articulate and uniquely compelling in her verbal expression she'd been—and conceivably, still was—and she frequently heard the young woman's voice in her head, memories of phrases spoken in her girl's pleasing syntax, the precise signifiers; and too, the baby's first sentence—spoken early, just after she'd taken her first steps: "I do it myself"—which she'd catalogued in her daughter's baby book, an album with an exterior patterned in pink stripes, a book she'd been proud of keeping for her daughter, something her own mother had never done for her.

Don't confuse amber with ambergris, that waxy waste product found in the intestines of the sperm whale (an endangered species), a solid substance valued as a fixative in perfumes, flotsam from deceased whales sought by beachcombers.

When her girl was ten years old, she'd moved her hundreds of miles away from where they'd both been born, a grimy town cold for much of the year, where her daughter's father had also lived (with his new family)—had moved her daughter as far south in Florida as they could possibly go, where they lived by the ocean and spent weekends by the water; the girl's eyes seeming to grow bluer in her glowing face now framed by sun-bleached curls, and her girl's (suddenly) long legs carrying her over the sand, sand that perpetually covered the floors of their apartment, sand they perpetually vacuumed from the cheap beige carpeting; and the girl missed her father, who never called.

Amber is the fossilized resin of trees from long-ago pine forests; when a tree became damaged, the resin seeped from the wound to harden, to become amber over a million years later.

Three years since the hang-up (which at this point in a life is a lifetime), and surely the girl's heart must harden with the passing time, for each foray she'd made to break the silence (emails, texts, voice messages, emailed photos—she no longer had a physical address for her daughter, though she'd heard she returned to the old town, to her father's house) had been met with silence.

Because it originates as a soft, sticky secretion, amber sometimes contains animal and plant material; inclusions such as insects, spiders and their webs, annelids, frogs, crustaceans, bacteria and amoebae, marine microfossils, wood, flowers and fruit, hair, feathers, and other small organisms have been recovered in Cretaceous ambers.

She'd been a girl herself when she'd had her daughter; she'd never wanted her girl to be so trapped—that's what her love was for, she'd thought; their terrible innocence was something they shared: she still believed that.

For amber, the Phoenicians (both hated and admired) traded salt, wine, dried fish, cedar, pine, metalwork, glass, embroidery, fine linen, and cloth dyed with the famous purple dye; their fine red-wheeled pottery, their ivory, and their storage jars containing wine and olive oil have been found far from their homelands.

Sometimes at night in bed, when her grief turned to anger, she allowed that, and on occasion (twice) said (as in *succumbed*, feeling petty and trite and ashamed) to her husband that she'd done nothing wrong—nothing!—and listed everything she'd wanted for and given her girl (what she'd never had): lessons in ballet, piano, violin; bicycles; the (despised) Barbies and accouterments; roller skates; art classes; sleepovers; parties; movies; dinners in restaurants; outings to the museums, symphony concerts, puppet shows and plays, parks, galleries, the (horrid) malls; books and journals; a phone; the fancy daybed with scrolled brasswork; the use of the car; and on and on, all acquired on her inadequate single mother's salary (the father was court-ordered to pay one hundred dollars a month the girl's entire childhood and had never contributed a cent more); but of course, of course she knows that she gave freely, that one can't expect that a person (her daughter, her beautiful daughter) might feel kindly in return—she doesn't want her daughter's allegiance out of a sense of duty: she just wants her daughter.

The Phoenicians pioneered the use of the pole star, enabling them to navigate at night.

In those days it had been hell going to college as a single mother, terrifying to move where she'd known no one and had no one in case of emergency, but it had all worked out and they had been happy, so happy, she'd thought then, and she was newly relieved and confused when recently she reunited with a coworker and friend from that time period, one whose expertise was in child development, who said of her daughter, *she was such a happy child* (if only she could call her girl and tell her that she'd met up with V again, a woman her girl had cared for).

The most notorious characteristic of the Phoenicians' religion was the practice of child sacrifice.

Not too long after her daughter had hung up on her, her girl posted on Facebook (before her daughter quit Facebook—a strange move that took place two years ago one autumn day, when out of the blue, her girl re-friended her, but before she could accept the request, her girl's page disappeared—which continued to grip her hard in the stomach when she thought of it, a gesture that might have been like throwing up a flare before going down on a sinking ship) a long proclamation about the nature of her forgiveness, how it had changed, saying that she had seen the light, and that post would have been hopeful except for the photo that accompanied it of the young woman with her father, her nose and eyes red, as if she'd been long crying.

The Phoenicians considered their warships living creatures and painted eyes on the ships' sides so that the vessels could guide the sailors through safe passageways.

What mother didn't want to believe that she'd done her best; wasn't it her fault that her daughter believed she could have done better, and what was it to make a common mistake that made for an unbearable consequence; to believe that she was permitted mistakes—wasn't that only the surface, an illusion, a mirror facing a mirror?

Some say amber possesses a unique aura that brings happiness, health, and prosperity.

She stood outside the jewelry store looking through the plate glass at a display of amber pendants in the cool afternoon, fog lying over the harbor at block's end, dreaming of her daughter beside her, her girl's face framed in the mirror set atop the display case, and asking her which necklace she liked, imagining how smooth the gem would feel to the touch, until the man inside stepped forward, close to the display, and smiled, his shadow falling over the case. She pushed her hand deep into her coat pocket, adjusted her collar to cover the back of her neck, and moved into the shrouding fog.

GLORY, CLOUD, AND EGG

THE CLOUD HOLDS SOME amount of the sea. All of the eggs of her daughter had been cradled within her too, the mother vessel. It's just science. In fifth grade music class she had been taught to sing: *in egg shells e day o.* The lesson recurs in the chamber of her mind randomly. The sea sound in the ears should you shape your empty palms around them, on its own, that sea sound swish is a sign of disease, of a blocked carotid artery. Across the country the cloud in her daughter's sky with its potion of ocean, the sea they each alone know in its obscured form. *Glo-o-o-o-o-O-o-o-o-o-O-o-o-o-o-O-ri-a in Ex-cel-sis De-o!*

STARFLOWER

[I WANT HER BACK]

SOMETIMES MY LONGING [DIRE] is to make myself very small and very quiet. [Thus reduced] I might slip myself into her life unnoticed. The world where lives my daughter. Veined sky domed over her fiery head; mossed path underfoot, sometimes the edge of a stone turned up. [To mark time passed. Passing.] If the universe should return her to me, never another false move to drive her away again. [As long as I live.] Drawing upon the subtle power of plants to heal, I sow swaths of purple flowered borage in the garden. Ah, bee bread! [Ornamental, edible, medicinal.] All day, each day the queens busy with the starflower. Sinuous wavy margins of the deep green leaves alternate up the stem. Hairy and rough. I would pluck and serve as a tea in her bone-white china cup. Cucumber flavor, light, a delight on my girl's tongue. [Her stilled tongue.] Each afternoon the drink. [Pliny the Elder recognized, advised. To give courage and comfort to the heart.] This self-seeder that will grow in highway ditches. Faring better in poor soils. Sometimes the flowers turn from blue to pink. Some times. [Time passing.] Blooms left alone produce excellent honey. [So sweet she must be. So sweet.]

AFTER MATH

THE BLOOD VOLUME OF most mammals is approximately seven to nine percent of ideal bodyweight: six to eight pints. Eight pints equals one gallon—she learned that in school, growing up. The bucket used to scrub the kitchen floor at home, after school, after math class, held two and one half gallons, but she filled it only partially with water because her thin arms couldn't lift a full bucket from the sink. The handle cut into her pale, ringless fingers.

Some details imprint themselves bodily, in the mind of the body, the body having a mind of its own.

The body will make a person do what it wants. Legs will fill with what they need to run, blood pumping pumping. Across the city a moon a shining low but unreachable beacon.

The young woman's blood spilled on the beige linoleum of the police station. Beside the red red pool, a sea—how many pints? It couldn't be a gallon—one of her flip-flops lay on its side. Where is the missing shoe? Where did it go?

Did the officer who documented this scene because he had to, because he couldn't get out of doing so, wonder that she was taken in the ambulance with one foot bare?

After the ER, head stitched closed, after she was given new pints of blood, after, where did the mind of her beaten body go?

CAVERN OBSCURA

THAT OLD EXPRESSION ABOUT the fox in the henhouse, she'd woken up thinking those words. Everywhere, the fog was thicker than where she stood on the rocky shoreline. The hissing and fizzing of the ocean below could beguile, and did. News reports lately of elaborate missions with helicopters to retrieve the bodies. Yesterday in the courtroom, when she'd taken her daughter's hand in hers, the hot flesh and bones, a primal circuitry fired in her brain. Her girl's hand, a young woman's burning soft hand. How long since her girl had been touched in comfort? Her daughter could tolerate but moments, hand going limp as if to make clear it was being held captive, and soon straining to be released—a sudden need to search through her purse. The purse, turquoise blue, big as a canyon, they'd shopped for it together the day before. That's what she could do: buy her daughter a pocketbook. Cavernous and mostly empty. But she knew the bag would fill quickly. Oh so rapidly. In the courtroom, only one more ending swept away when the judge ordered the girl's husband to prison. The tide would come rushing back in. Spindrift hidden under fog. Unseen creatures on their silent feet, doing what they must.

~NINE~

THE LITTLE GIRL, WHOM SHE
CARRIED ON HER BACK, WAS
A WILD AND RECKLESS CREATURE

THE CAKE IS
IN THE GARDEN

IT HAS NO MIND of its own. Whoever wants takes a piece of it. This frivolous, pretty thing, mindless and aging in the sun. And sweet. In the heat, sugars separating. The inevitable decline. Remains left for the bugs and beasts.

AN ANIMAL IN
THE HIGHER ORDER

SOME DAYS SHE WANTED to be nothing more than the animal she was, acting on instinct. Other times she wanted to feel gratitude for the distinguishing characteristic of her species. She liked the science that defined the nature of animals, but when she heard the phrase *animal kingdom* she couldn't help but picture little crowns and tiaras sparkling on the heads of squirrels, mice, starlings—images of animals so cuddly cute, they might peacefully be held in her lap, communing joyfully, when of course this wasn't representative of the Way Things Are.

It was difficult to be the animal in the higher order. All the thinking! Thoughts would not let her alone. Robins hopped over her front lawn pecking their meals from the ground before swooping away. No second guessing. No complicated strategizing. No self-blame. Governed solely by instinct.

All mammals, birds, fish, reptiles, amphibians, even invertebrates slept. Sleep was integral to animal life. Which wren, which seal, which gecko, trout, cobra jerked awake night after night to toss and turn in its nest, hollow, hole, as she did in her bed? Which arose to walk the house in a haze, coming awake to find oneself standing in the middle of stairs, say, and wondering where one was going and why? She reveled in a vision of the meadow vole curled up in its underground chamber as adorable, yet at the same time she was dismayed at the mind that construed a wild animal as a pet, subject to her benevolence.

Who would she be without this mind?

It was as if the deepest part of her wished to escape, trekking her house each night, wandering the rooms, following some lost call, rather than moving through a place of remembrance.

An animal was judged to be asleep when it displayed typical sleep posture (lying down); inactivity of voluntary muscles (her legs heavy on the tangled covers); a lack of responsiveness to typical external stimuli (the man with his probing fingers); and quick reversibility of the unconscious state with intense stimulation (her eyes flew open at his bite).

Science deemed a dream the mind's attempt to interpret random firings within the brain without the imposition of logical reasoning, allowing the human animal to defy the laws of gravity. Each night her legs, abandoned by the prefrontal cortex's ordering of chaos, believed themselves wings. Each night, flight.

EXPOSED

AFTER THE HOUSEKEEPER LEAVES, she immediately checks the photograph of her grandmother that sits on the sofa table in the shining, empty silence. Though she's spoken to the housekeeper several times about it, still the woman is careless with the old picture, its rickety wooden frame, the sepia photo long ago adhered to the glass.

As some detect the ghosts of disapproving ancestors, she senses her grandmother's presence in the house, a place her grandmother never visited. In life, her grandmother both approved and disapproved of her, of the way she rushed headlong into experiences. The way she wanted to know what lay underneath. The way she was drawn to the shadows formed under fallen leaves.

Her grandmother warned her, you can't live with a man and not be lonely. Her grandmother had been taken in herself, by the poetry on her grandfather's tongue. When she said this, her eyes filled with a piquant sadness, the kind that comes with the knowledge that nothing good can ever last. Even at the end, in her hospital bed, her faded green eyes bore that understanding. Keep going anyhow, her grandmother seemed to say, a papery hand cool on hers.

Isn't that the message of the photograph on the table, the picture she's moved from house to house—some houses shared with a man, some not. No longer pushing at the edges of life trying to turn up anything. She protects the photo as she can, a picture that was never meant to be kept in a drawer. A picture that must live in the burn of the air, subject to sunlight, exposed.

TANGLED CORDS AND NESTING DOLLS

C OLOR THEORY IS A body of practical guidance (in the visual arts). At the high school reunion, her classmate, face blazing above her red blouse, expressed anger over the ineptitude of their high school guidance counselors: her whole life could have been different had a counselor suggested the availability of college scholarships. Railroad tracks ran through the southern end of the town where she'd grown up. Night is a lonely time, when most people are asleep, even those on trains passing through villages, fields, forests. At first some people may develop headaches when they stop drinking coffee, but not headaches so severe as to cause their field of vision to go white.

In the morning her senses were most acute: she smelled the wild perfume of an unknown shrub close to her open window, the beloved mustiness of her husband's empty side of the bed, and soon would come the sharp odor of his soap from the shower. She had been eight years old when her father took the job he'd retire from, repairing broken machinery, work that he counterbalanced with watching TV all weekend, the sound of the excited sportscasters loud throughout the house usually giving her headaches that chained her to the top of her bed where she lay with eyes closed against the yellow-checked quilt.

For years after she was married, she used to love roaming through antique malls on a Sunday afternoon with her husband, until one day, gazing at a heap of old beige office telephones, their dirty tangled cords sprawled like the innards of dead animals, she felt something cold settle into the pit of her stomach, and knew she wanted no more evidence of anyone's past. The cowbird lays its eggs in the nests of other birds, where if the egg survives, the newly hatched baby is fed like a foster child alongside the true hatchlings. How much her father had liked her high school classmate—at the sight of the girl's green eyes sparkling in her rosy face, his jaw softened, the ends of his mouth curved almost into a smile.

The ocean is always in motion, its color a reflection of the sky above. There's little to which one can apply the qualifiers *always* or *never*, but it's true that she had never learned to whistle, a trivial matter in the larger scheme of things, unworthy of shame, and yet. Scientists using mice to study fertility (she pictures white mice, like the ones in her kindergarten classroom) have discovered that the creatures are able to produce new eggs later in life when their egg follicles are destroyed. Once her daughter had told her with a tone of hushed reverence that because women were born with all the eggs they would ever produce in their lifetimes, that meant that when she'd been pregnant with her daughter, she'd also been carrying inside too all her future grandchildren (like Russian nesting dolls, painted blue babushkas on their heads)—and oh, how she'd loved that magical idea, most of all because of how happy it made her daughter to believe in the connection.

Unless one dies first, the fiftieth birthday is inevitable. Each night for the long weekend celebration, she gorged herself on the sugary cake her husband had ordered from an expensive bakery, the thick buttercream frosting ornate with pastel pink petals and red raspberry filling, and felt pity for her poor body that would have to carry her through the hurtful caper, wondering when her body would simply call it quits.

KEEPING

S HE STOOD ON THE stool in the kitchen to reach the top shelf where she remembered the jar of hazelnuts to be. She wanted to try a new recipe, make a smoothie for breakfast. God knows why. She stood in her thick fuzzy socks, anklets of pale blue, on the solid stool, her warm fleece robe tied close, keeping out the morning chill. Just before, she'd closed all the windows left open through the night. Since she used the hazelnuts so rarely, they were high in the cupboard. Had they kept, she wondered, her hand sweeping the shelf, when her phone dinged in the pocket of her robe, startling her.

Fast and slow she fell to the floor, the wooden stool toppling over, too—a bang on the head that truly stunned her. Moments passed. Or a lifetime. (Her girl, her long lost girl—a kaleidoscope of savored images cycled through her mind: blonde braids, graceful hand on the violin bow, enigmatic smile on the driver's license photo.) When next she could feel, there was the cold on her breasts, her belly—her robe flung open. Something else new and unfamiliar, a pain pulsing through her leg bent underneath her. That throb above the temple.

Her hand trembled, searching through the fleecy fabric of her robe for the phone. The modern lifeline. Help was at hand. But the folds of the robe were slack. No shape to grasp. She managed, with exertion, to lift her head, to turn it, sharp pangs in her ribs cutting into her breath. Down the length of the galley kitchen she spotted the phone, the dark blank glossy face.

Oh what a story! She, a woman of agency, reduced to this character subject to fickleness, to felicity. No one cares about a character like that. Especially not a woman—a woman can no longer afford to be anything less than the heroine of her own story.

Oh get up, get up. She laughed and laughed until she wept, and wept, and could not let herself think of how long it would be until someone thought to think of her, a woman who enjoyed her solitude, who kept to herself: how long would she keep?

BURNING

MY PARENTS' EYES RESTED on me, when I was a child, weighing the matter from their distance of authority. That was what it was to be theirs. They believed they knew me better than I knew myself. Even my mind seemed to belong to them up to a certain age. *I can read you like a book.*

That I did not think what they thought I thought was my dark secret, one that could fill me with guilt. While, still, at times I feared they did know what I was thinking and they would not be pleased. *Don't give me that look.*

Stars fell into the lake, hissing, clotting. Sometimes I wished that they did know what I was thinking, for though they would not rest a gentle hand on my head, I would be less lonely. The moon poured its light into a lake on the other side of the world.

My parents were one, a unit, in their commitment to making me. To leave home, unformed, a young person, was to burn far away, the way some stars must, not wanting to exist in the same sky with the others.

But a life gets lived, a mind becomes one's own, perhaps, while no one's watching. *She's got a mind of her own.*

Some starless nights I wander the streets once the moon has set, houses crouched in the dark, harmless, unseeing. My parents' eyes assessing the worth of me, their child they'd made: I don't want to forget that feeling. When I do, it will mean they are all the way gone.

NOTE TO A GHOST

AFTER YOU DIED I wandered the nearby field. Twilight. Your cat ran up to me with a bird's heart in its mouth. I wanted to make something more out of that than what it was. You know what it was. The way you knew to let out your first cry: how you were there and not, how it's a witness who hears and translates raw sensation voiced in the tone. It's only natural, as in leaves abandoning the trees to fall at your feet, as is the bleeding red moon this night, scientifically explicable. Beast, bird, botany, being—all knowable.

ACKNOWLEDGMENTS

I CAN'T BEGIN TO name everyone who has been so important to me in writing this book, and I'm sure to later remember others I ought to have mentioned.

I am grateful to the editors of the following publications, in which portions of this book first appeared, sometimes in slightly different versions.

Waxwing: "A Girl Goes Into the Forest," "Smoke, Must, Dust," "Crucible of History," and "Unknown Animals"; *Your Impossible Voice*: "Old Church by the Sea"; *Helen Literary Magazine*: "Iguana"; *Tupelo Quarterly*: "An Uncle"; *Sugar Mule*: "Your Spree in Paris"; *Permafrost*: "My Father and His Slim Beautiful Brunettes"; *Scoundrel Time*: "Pond Water," "Friendliness," "Geniuses," and "After Math"; *Healdsburg Center for the Arts Shadows and Reflections Exhibition Catalogue*: "His Apartment in the City"; *Blotterature*: "Our Losses"; *VOLT*: "Day Lilies" and "Green Glass Bird"; *Forklift Ohio*: "Abandoning the Birds" and "Burning"; *Entropy Magazine*: "Baby Bird"; *The Gravity of the Thing*: "In the Beginning"; *you are here: the journal of creative geography*: "House in the Desert"; *Soundings Review*: "Wedding Gift"; Audible, "Wedding Gift"; *The Negatives*: "Love Carnival";

Connotation Press: "Laundry," "Schematics," and "Exposed"; *Bending Genres:* "Rust"; *Mom Egg Review:* "Glory, Cloud, and Egg" and "Starflower [I Want Her Back]"; *b(OINK):* "Cavern Obscura"; *100 Word Stories* and *Nothing Short Of: Selected Stories of 100 Word Stories:* "Note to a Ghost."

This book owes a debt of gratitude to "The Snow Queen" by Hans Christian Andersen, first published December 1844 in *New Fairy Tales.* The fairy tale furnishes each section's epigraph. Wikipedia (!) provided information for "An Ancient Trade."

Deepest thanks to Michelle Dotter, editor of Dzanc Books, for saying yes to this book and articulating its vision and quest, for her intelligent and insightful reading and edits, and for her indefatigable work on behalf of this collection. It's impossible to say how much her support has mattered during these dark times in this country.

Thank you to the artist Matthew Revert, who created this perfect book cover.

Thank you forever to Karen Brennan, Kevin McIlvoy, Christian Kiefer, Marisa Silver, Ramona Ausubel, and Karen E. Bender. To Joan Silber, Margot Livesey, and Chuck Wachtel. Endless gratitude to Ellen Bryant Voigt, always. To Tamim Ansary, Lauren Alwan, Nancy Au, Mari Coates, Joan Frank, Scott Landers, Louise Marburg, Kate Milliken, Ron Nyren, John Philipp, Bora Reed, Charles Smith, Sarah Stone, Robert Thomas, Genanne Walsh, Olga Zilberbourg.

I'm so grateful to the organization and community that is WTAW. You buoy me and make me remember how what we do matters, that joy is its own form of resistance. Michael Collins, Michael DuBon, Haldane King, Nancy Koerbel, Maggie Pahos, Linda Michel-Cassidy, Alison Moore, Patrick O'Neil, Ashley Perez, Barbara Roether, Lisa Gluskin Stonestreet, and Virginia Bellis.

Thank you, Dr. Christine Blasey Ford—and every woman who has braved and risked so much to be heard, to speak their truths to power.

Love and thanks to my family, especially to my mother who modeled her love of reading: I can't remember ever not knowing that she loved to read; and to my father, who valued and made it possible for us to have the daily paper, magazines, and books in our house when I was a girl. A bonfire burns in my heart for Cathy, Katie, and Jason, who have always gone out of their ways to love me back.

Endless love and gratitude to Cass Pursell. I always knew you were out there.